T0128803

"MARINE" I AM ONE

"*MARINE*" *I AM ONE*

Book Two in a War Trilogy

Charles Giezentanner

"MARINE" I AM ONE
BOOK TWO IN A WAR TRILOGY

iUniverse books may be ordered through booksellers or by contacting:

iUniverse
1663 Liberty Drive
Bloomington, IN 47403
www.iuniverse.com
1-800-Authors (1-800-288-4677)

Because of the dynamic nature of the Internet, any web addresses or links contained in this book may have changed since publication and may no longer be valid. The views expressed in this work are solely those of the author and do not necessarily reflect the views of the publisher, and the publisher hereby disclaims any responsibility for them.

Any people depicted in stock imagery provided by Thinkstock are models, and such images are being used for illustrative purposes only. Certain stock imagery © Thinkstock.

ISBN: 978-1-5320-0529-9 (sc)
ISBN: 978-1-5320-0528-2 (e)

Library of Congress Control Number: 2016913825

Print information available on the last page.

iUniverse rev. date: 10/05/2016

CONTENTS

To my dear FRIEND and MENTOR, Charles Javens, PHD.

His encouragement and friendship has made
this novel possible…

CHAPTER 1

Coming to America

Franz was the youngest of the four Charles children their father, Herbert (pronounced A-bear), a widower, brought from Switzerland to America for a better life. The family arrived at Ellis Island in New York in 1906, and no one in the family could speak English. The Irish employees and officials at the immigration office decided that New York had enough non-English-speaking Jews, so they put the Jews on trains to be dropped off in southern cities.

The train was crowded. The family had no food, water, or toilets. Herbert Charles had his three boys surround Etta, his only daughter, to keep her as safe as they could on the train.

As soon as the train traveled over the Mason-Dixon Line, the conductors started putting families off in each city that the train stopped at. By the time the train got to Johnson City, Tennessee, where the Charles family was put off, it was mostly empty of immigrants.

The family was lost in a town they had never seen in a country in which they did not speak the language, and they had no money. Herbert took his family to a church. He motioned to the minister with his hands to his mouth and then to his stomach that they were hungry. He made sweeping motions as if to say he would clean the church in payment.

The minister could tell the family was in trouble. He led Herbert and the children to the parsonage and told his wife to feed them. She served them corn bread, fatback, green beans, and stewed turnips that were hot and good. Afterward, the minister led the family to his barn and in sign language let them know they could spend the night there.

The following morning, the minister brought the family biscuits, jam, fried fatback, and stewed apples that were good and filling. The minister pointed to himself and said, "Tom." He pointed to Herbert, who said "E-bear."

The minister pointed to the children one by one and learned their names and ages. Otto was ten, John was seven, Etta was five, and Franz was two.

The minister took Herbert to the horse stall and gave him a shovel. By the time the minister got back that afternoon, the barn and the stalls were clean and everything had been stacked very neatly. Herbert had brushed, cleaned, and fed the horse and the mule, and he had fed the chickens and gathered the eggs. The minister was quite pleased.

That evening, the minister's wife came to the barn and sat out a large picnic for the Charles family of deviled eggs, fried chicken, baked beans with onions, biscuits, and a large pecan pie. While the family ate, Mrs. Hamilton sat behind little Etta and combed and brushed her hair, and she gave her some hair bows.

The next morning, the minister served the family breakfast in the barn again and explained with hand signals for Herbert to follow him to the next farm over. Herbert was to clean that barn and chicken house in return for food.

Herbert worked very hard that day, and the farmer gave him enough food for the family for two days. Herbert and Otto had already picked up some English—*food, hello, good, work,* and *good-bye.* He asked Herbert if he could dig a cesspool. Herbert said yes. Herbert said good-bye to the minister and his wife and moved his family into the farmer's barn.

The farmer's wife gave Herbert a pot, a frying pan, and some cooking utensils. The farmer led Herbert to the woods behind his house and showed him an old corncrib that the family could use as its home. Herbert shook the farmer's hand and said, "Thank you."

That is where the family set up housekeeping. It wasn't much, but it was dry and safe. That night, Herbert played his violin. He felt happy for the first time in months.

For the next few days, he and Otto walked from farm to farm to pick up work, and they fixed up their new home; they cleaned it and patched the holes in it. Each day, Herbert would put down some flooring until he had a complete hardwood floor. It was beginning to look like a home.

The family soon had plenty of food and lots of work. Herbert taught Otto and John to trap rabbits and squirrels, and the boys learned to fish and cook. He taught them to pick berries and fruit. Herbert developed a reputation for being a hard, honest worker and got jobs in the town and on the farms. He and Otto worked in the sawmill and on the railroad.

Herbert built a henhouse for a couple in town, and they gave him an old guitar, which he taught Otto and John to play. Herbert was trying to teach Etta the violin as he had taught Otto and John, but Franz was still too young to learn to play the instruments.

After a year and a half of living in the corncrib, Herbert met Stella Carter, a spinster of about forty who had a farm that was becoming run-down; she needed someone to work it. She was the daughter of a Free Church minister and his wife, a schoolteacher. Stella was one of three children; she had stayed in Jonesboro and had never married, unlike her siblings. She had elected to stay on the farm and take care of her parents in their later years, and she had inherited the farm after her parents died.

It was fifteen acres of rocks and dirt. It had a sharecropper's home on it, a home where Stella lived, a barn, a chicken house, a carriage house, and an outhouse. It was not much of a farm, but a couple of streams ran through it, and they were full of brown trout.

Stella was a good, handsome woman pretty well off by Jonesboro standards. She and Herbert fell in love and married a year after he went to work for her. She became a real mother to his children. She loved them, and they loved her. Herbert taught piano, guitar, and violin to children in the area and was offered a job teaching music and music equipment repair at a Baptist College in Mars Hill, North Carolina, which he accepted. Stella took the job as a cook at the woman's dorm at the college.

CHAPTER 2

Mars Hill College

So Herbert's family moved into faculty housing with indoor plumbing and three bedrooms. The family was living the American dream that all immigrants sought. The children were in school and learning and playing music—all but Franz. He was six and did not seem to have an ear for music. He was a bit of a bully at school; he was smart but did not show it.

He liked to hang around with the faster crowds, the ne'er-do-wells, the dandies. Herbert had to watch Franz at church when they passed the offering plate because Franz was very good at palming some of the change as the plates would pass by.

At age eight, Franz was caught peeing in the birdbaths around campus. At nine, he was caught smoking. At ten, peeking in to the ladies' changing room at the gym. Franz became a marble hustler; he won all the other boys' marbles and would sell them back to the losers. Franz was the man to go to on the campus if the students needed cigarettes, cigars, or candy. He also made money pitching pennies with the students. By the time Franz was twelve, he knew all the latest dances and songs, he loved hanging out on the campus, and he loved looking at and talking to the coeds.

Stella and Herbert refused to take Franz to town with them; he was bound to put things in his pockets or sometimes take a bite of something and put it back on the shelf. One time when Herbert took Franz to the hardware store, he saw Franz setting mousetraps to antagonize unsuspecting customers. Franz kept letting the air out of the tires on the police cars. He would change road signs and send people in circles. He put a mustache on the baby Jesus and a cigar in the mouth of Joseph in the Christmas display on the church lawn.

The whole town of Mars Hill and the college knew that if trouble happened, it was Franz; they just could never prove it. Herbert wondered if living out in the woods those three years had messed up Franz's brain. All Franz would read were crime magazines, dime novels, and the *Police Gazette.*

He always told everybody that if he had lived in the Old West, he would have been the best gunfighter there. He put a hand-cranked police siren on his bicycle and would ride through the campus in the middle of the night with siren blaring. He liked to ride by weddings and funerals with the siren going as well. Herbert had to lock up Franz's bike before the townspeople ran them out of town.

When the college had its yearly Christmas gift exchange with all the professors and their families with desserts and coffee and tea, Franz snuck into the great hall and changed most of the gift tags. That evening, when the president of the college dressed as Santa Claus and started handing out the gifts, children got adult gifts, women got men's gifts, and some adults got children's gifts. All the children were crying, and everybody knew Franz was to blame. Herbert had to take him home early.

Herbert told everybody that Franz had fallen into a hornets' nest in Jonesboro and had gotten stung so many times; he said that was probably why Franz was so mean. What had really happened was that Franz had tried to knock down the hornets' nest at a church revival and the hornets got him instead of the worshipers.

Franz missed his big brother, Otto, who had gotten a job with the railroad and had married and moved to Sweetwater, Tennessee. Otto was about the only one Franz had ever listened to.

For the next five years, the Charles family had it rough with Franz being the way he was. He would use his neighbors' tomatoes for batting practice and use their green peppers as targets for his slingshot. He would catch rats, squirrels, and raccoons and lock them in people's cars.

He started going into dorm rooms while students were in class and taking any money he could find. Franz would steal coeds' panties and sell them to the male students. The county sheriff arrested Franz for running a small bookie operation on campus and a loan shark business when he was not quite fifteen.

It was 1918, and the war to end all wars was going on in Europe. The judge of Madison County told the Charles family that Franz went either into the army or jail. Herbert and Stella signed him up with the army.

Franz did not seem to care if he went into the army or jail; they were both the same to him. Physically, Franz was in great shape; he was young but the same size as the other men in the army. He went through basic training without any trouble, and most of the men in his company owed him money from gambling by the time he finished basic training.

He was assigned to a language school in New Orleans and taught simple German to combat troops getting ready to go to Europe. Franz did not have to go to Europe because the army was not sure which side he would fight on. And he was just too young to go overseas to fight.

Franz loved New Orleans. He made friends with the restaurant owners and the chefs, with the musicians, and with the gamblers. Franz was six foot and built very well; he combed his black hair back and dressed like a million bucks.

He was a ferocious street fighter. He liked to pick fights with the college students when he lived in Mars Hill, and he became very good at taking down much older and bigger opponents. He learned to never give up in a fight, to fight until one of the combatants could not fight anymore. He learned to use a knife very well. He also picked up cooking and sewing skills and refined his dating and dancing skills.

Franz seemed to have a knack for gambling; he learned to cheat at cards. He was promoted three times to Private first class, but with all the fights and schemes and hustling, he was busted back to slick-sleeve Private every time. But he did not care. He always had money, so he dressed very well and learned to tailor his cloths so they fit like a glove.

Franz was a skilled lover; he had learned that art at Mars Hill College not as a student but as the campus stud. He had his first lesson in lovemaking with one of the colored dishwashers at the cafeteria in the women's dorm. He learned to prey on young coeds who were vulnerable because of a love lost, or being away from home and scared, or because of a death in the family. He was always there like a vulture. Herbert had said that Franz was the way he was because Franz has lost his mother early in life and did not know how to respect women. Either that or that he was just worthless.

Franz spent the last six months of his tour of duty in the army in the brig, having gotten into a fight with some British sailors. It happened when the British accused him of cheating in a blackjack game, which he had been doing, but he did not like anyone saying he cheated. The fight was four to one, but Franz, with the help of his hawk-billed knife, bested all four. He took their money and decided to leave a message for everyone not to mess with him. He cut Xs on their foreheads.

The army was glad to see Franz go. He stayed in New Orleans and worked at clubs and gambling houses. In January 1920, the Volstead Act became law, and alcoholic beverages were prohibited, so Franz found a lot of work with the bootleggers, and he helped set up illegal speakeasies with gambling. He became the head collector for a couple of gamblers, a job he could do and he liked very well because he got to use his physical skills as well as his brains.

He loved his life and lifestyle. He learned to cook like a European top chef in the restaurants and bordellos of New Orleans, he learned how to look and act like a very educated gentleman, he learned about weapons and how to use them, and he learned to pick locks and crack safes.

In 1928, Franz turned twenty-five. He started to travel to different places—Cuba, Miami, Rio de Janeiro, and the Texas and Alabama coasts. He loved traveling. He looked and talked like a European royal or maybe even an American actor or a very successful businessman. He stayed in only the best places and went to only the best clubs. He learned to play golf and then how to hustle golf.

CHAPTER 3

Cuba

On one trip to Cuba, Franz was invited to a cockfight; he had seen plenty of them in Madison County and all around New Orleans but nothing like what he saw in Cuba. The referees wore red shirts with white neckerchiefs. They had beer stands. They had betting booths. Men, women, and children would have a great time at the fights.

Once, Franz spilled a beer on a man at the betting booth. He was Franz's height but very skinny. He was colored with red hair. He gave Franz a stare that actually kind of scared Franz, and that was very hard to do. Franz nodded to the man and bowed his head. The man just looked and turned his back on Franz. Franz thought, *I have the feeling I need to filet this man right now because I know I'm going to run into him again and he may not be as nice next time.* Franz left for his hotel.

The next day, Franz learned of a new game he could bet on, jai alai, a game he had never even heard of much less seen played. He had dinner at the hotel with other guests who were from New York—three gentlemen and five ladies who seemed to be kin to each other. They had great Cuban food—-conch salad, black beans, red rice, fried bananas, and great steaks.

Franz and the group went to the jai alai stadium. It was large and very crowded. The stadium was very modern, first class. All the people were dressed in their best—men in suits and tuxes and women in formal dresses. Everyone was drinking champagne and betting heavily. Franz headed to the betting cages and the first person he saw was the red-haired Cuban. He was in a cheap tux and was with a very beautiful

Cuban woman. *I knew I was going to run into this man again. Now what do I do?*

Franz remembered the man drank beer. He saw that the man did not have anything to drink, so he went to the bar and ordered two beers. He took the beers to the red-haired gentleman and wanted to say, "Would you like a beer?" but he did not speak Spanish, so he just handed him the beer.

The man looked at Franz for a moment and smiled. "Gracias."

Franz smiled and bowed. *That was easy.*

The man looked at Franz and said in a southern accent, "Are you an American?"

"Yep. How about you?"

"Sure am." He stuck out his hand. "Isaiah Green."

Franz took his hand. "Franz Charles."

They shook hands and laughed.

"Man, I thought you were some kind of Cuban gangster," said Isaiah.

Franz laughed. "I thought the same thing about you."

They laughed again.

"I detect a southern accent," Isaiah said. "Where are you from?"

"I was born in Switzerland, moved as a child to the mountains of Tennessee, then as a young boy moved to Mars Hill, North Carolina. My dad is a music teacher there. What about you?"

"Man, I'm from Asheville, North Carolina, about two towns east of Mars Hill."

"I know where that is. It's a big city compared to Mars Hill."

Isaiah was about ten years older than Franz, but they hit it off like long-lost buddies. They drank and bet on jai alai most of the evening. They both lost but had a great time.

The stadium started closing. Isaiah and Franz left together. Outside, Franz said, "I really need to pee."

"Go in the alley," said Isaiah. "I'll watch for you."

As Franz was reliving himself, he heard someone say, "Turn around slowly and hand me your money."

"You got the wrong guy, Mister," Franz said. "I lost. I have no money." He slowly turned and was trying to zip up.

"Leave it out and hand me your wallet. You Americans always have money."

Franz saw that the man wore a police uniform and held a very large machete. Franz understood why the man had said to leave it out. There was no way Franz would try to jump the man with his thing hanging out and with the man having a machete.

As Franz reached for his wallet, he saw Isaiah put his hand over the policeman's mouth and stab him in the back a few times.

Isaiah let the man drop to the ground. "Let's go before his friends come looking for him."

Both men walked briskly away.

"Thanks, man, for watching my back. That damn cop could have made a soprano out of me."

"Don't mention it," replied Isaiah. "I really mean don't ever mention it again."

"No problem."

"Does it bother you what I just had to do?" asked Isaiah.

"Doesn't bother me. I think he deserved it."

"Good. Good."

They walked in silence.

As they got close to a hotel, Franz pointed at it. "That's mine."

Isaiah nodded. "I'm down the street."

Franz said, "I going deep-sea fishing tomorrow. Would you like to come along and fish? We have plenty of room."

Isaiah shrugged. "Sure. I've never been deep-sea fishing before. Sounds like fun."

"We'll meet here at my hotel at six this morning. Don't be late," said Franz.

Isaiah waved to Franz. "I'll be here, and I'm always on time."

At six the next morning, Franz came into the lobby and saw Isaiah in dress pants and a white shirt and nice but cheap black shoes. He was wearing a fedora. Franz just shook his head. It was too late to tell him to change clothes because deep-sea fishing was not the cleanest sport in the world. Franz and Isaiah and three other men walked to the docks.

There were rows and rows of fishing boats for tourists. The fishermen had coolers of beer and baskets of sandwiches. Franz's group stopped at one boat and started boarding. As the boat started its engines and pulled out, Isaiah was excited; he had never been on a boat on the ocean before and had never fished for anything of any size. The biggest fish he had ever caught was eleven pounds; these men were talking about not keeping anything under forty pounds.

Isaiah saw deck chairs with seat belts bolted to the floor and wondered, *Are the fish big enough to pull you into the ocean? Why the hell did I agree to this?*

The fishing boat gunned its engines. A crewman on their boat started serving beers. Isaiah was fine for about twenty minutes. As long as the boat was speeding along, it was not bad, but when they slowed and started to troll for fish, the boat rocked back and forth, and Isaiah started getting seasick. He could feel beer sloshing around in his stomach. He threw up over the rail and started in with the dry heaves. He asked Franz if they could take him back to Cuba. Franz told him that the trip was going to be eight hours and they could not go back to port.

The Captain and the mate laughed. "I have something that will help him," the mate said. He gave Isaiah a hand-rolled cigarette and showed him how to smoke it. It did not smell like tobacco, but Isaiah smoked it any way. He became real mellow and asked for a sandwich. He just sat and giggled.

Franz ask the Captain was kind of cigarette that was.

The Captain laughed. "Ganja."

"What's that?" asked Franz.

"Reefer, weed, you know, man," replied the mate.

"No I don't know. Isaiah, do you know what he's talking about?" Franz asked.

Isaiah laughed. "Yeah, man, I know what he's talking about, but I've never tried it until now, and boy, I'm glad I did. I may be able to finish this fishing trip now. I'm not going to fish. I'm just going to lie here, eat, and relax."

Isaiah was quite happy for the rest of the trip. Each of the men caught fish, but only two caught anything big enough to keep, and both of them were not Franz.

When the fishing trip was over, Franz had to help Isaiah to his hotel room. Franz told Isaiah to take a nap, he would be back at eight to pick him up for dinner. Isaiah waved and lay on the bed as happy as he could be.

As Franz left Isaiah's hotel, he told the desk clerk to make sure Isaiah was up by seven fifteen.

"Sir, I won't be here at seven fifteen in the morning," responded the clerk.

"No, I mean tonight, seven fifteen tonight." He gave the man a peso.

When he returned to Isaiah's hotel, he saw Isaiah in the same cheap tux he had been wearing when Franz met him. Franz could smell an inexpensive aftershave on Isaiah and his tux. His shoes were not the patent-leather type normally worn with a tux but cheap shoes that were not shined.

Franz picked a middle-of-the-road restaurant, not wanting to embarrass Isaiah by taking him to a first-class place. The men talked and drank most of the night away. Isaiah told Franz he had to leave in a couple days for a job he'd been hired to do in Miami. A rich Jewish man owned a bar with a bookie joint in the back and needed a colored man to run it. It was in a seedy part to town, and the Jewish man had gotten too old to run it safely. He had hired Isaiah when he heard Isaiah was an honest bookie. Isaiah would get half the money they made. Isaiah asked Franz, "Why don't you come with me? You said you liked Miami, and you said you were kind of without of a job, so why not?"

"Sounds like a plan to me," replied Franz.

CHAPTER 4

Mr. Daddy Rabbit..

Isaiah Green
1897

"**R**un, run get into that hole fast." [The hole was a hole in the wooden floor of a share croppers shack in the town of Meridian Mississippi. The colored share croppers were always in fear of the white red necks getting drunk and coming to beat them, rob them, rape them and on occasions hang one of the male coloreds. A lot of the shared croppers had hiding places for them and their children for just these times. Under the floor of their share cropper homes, under the floor of the farm equipment in the barn, or in a hidden hole out in the woods around the farm.] "Run, run chillien, hide and don't make a sound," cried Mrs. Janie Green, "run, run, please hurry."

Mrs. Janie's Green's husband, Mr. Big Abe Green, [*named after President Abraham Lincoln*] started running from the barn to his house as soon as he heard the red necks drive up in a truck and on horse back. He was going to try to help and protect his family. Three of the drunken white southern boys who were in an old Army flat bed truck one of them had bought at an Army surplus auction in Meridian. They drove the truck between Big Abe Green and his home. Abe tried to run around the truck but the red necks keep blocking him with the truck.

"Hey, we need some help back here, this is a big buck, too big for us to try to handle alone. Don't let him get to the house, I hear that he has a shot gun in the house," cried one of the white boys.

Big Abe Green did not have a shot gun nor any other kind of a weapon. Big Abe could fire a weapon. He was taught in the United States Army. Big Abe joined the Army during the "Spanish American War," to help feed his family. He became part of Black Jack Pershing's Calvary troop. Black Jack Pershing led a company of American Buffalo Soldiers to Cuba in the Spanish American War. Big Abe's time in the Army was in the Rough Riders in Cuba and in the Philippians, where he worked in the stables and new motor pool. [*colored men were only allowed to worked in the kitchens, laundry, stables, and the new motor pools, and as hospital orderly's after the Spanish American War.*]where his was taught him to clean and groom horses and mules and he was taught to work on the new motor cars and trucks engine parts with red devil lye and machine oil.

After the war in Cuba was over, close to half the colored American cavalry men stayed in Cuba, and a large group of the other colored soldiers went with Pershing to the Philippians for that year, and Abe was one of those men who went to the Philippians. After his time was up and he was discharged from the Army, and he went back to Meridian Mississippi to his share cropper's farm and to his wife Janie and his three son's, ages, four, five ,and six,. He was only home nine months when Janie gave him a beautiful little girl, called Lizzie. Big Abe settled into farming of the crops and also repairing farm equipment for other share croppers. Each year Janie gave him another child, two more boys and another girl, Abe had seven beautiful children in all.

Three other white boys on horse back came riding around the house and also blocked Big Abe. Abe's second son was Isaiah Green, aged ten.. Young Isaiah crawled under the house to a place where he could see out but could not be seen. He had on his sleeping cloths on, a pair of under shorts and a large shirt. The white boys tried to grab Big Abe, but he threw the first boy who tried to jump him from his back over the back of the truck. One of the boys on horse back tried to run Abe down with the horse but Abe dodged the horse.

Abe's oldest son, eleven year old Joe Don, dressed on ly in a pair of under shorts, slid from the crawl space to the front of the house, he stayed low to the ground and he tried to run to the corner of the cotton crop. Two other of the drunken white boys jumped from their horses and caught young Joe Don.

The oldest of the drunken boys say's to his brother, Ottis, the other white boy, "let see if this nigger can run, you know that they have animal blood in them, hand me that rope." He then put the rope around Joe Don's neck, "don't worry nigger, this ain't no noose, I ain't gonn'a hang you, we're just gonn'a see how fast you can run, you wanna run, don't, don't you boy?" Laughed Delbert "This boy's ready to show us if he can run."

The white boy, Ottis, jumped on his horse and said, "lets go nigger, start running. Do you think that the TNT, tattooed on my hand, it don't say explosive, no it say's, trot Nigger trot." Otis started laughing.

Big Abe saw what the two brothers were doing and he ran to help his son, "leave him a lone, I said, leave him alone." Big Abe kept running to the place the white trash boy's had Joe Don. "Let my boy go you white trash."

The white men in the truck saw a chance to knock Big Abe to the ground by hitting him solid in the back with the truck as he ran to help his son. The men hit him, "got him, now that he's down, put the noose around his neck and put the other end up into that tree. Now tie the loose end to the bumper of this truck," hollered the leader of the group of drunken white men. "Hurry up before he comes too, he'll be hell to handle then," He added.

The other white men and boy's did as they we're told to do, they were laughing like this was all a game.

Janie, Big Abe's wife ran out of the house to stop the hanging of her husband. She ran screaming Big Abe's name. "Abe, Abe. wake up Abe, wake up"

Isaiah had crawled over to another watching spot to see what was happening. He saw his big brother Joe Don was still tied to a horse and he was still laying on the ground crying for his Father.

The two boys on the horses with Joe Don on the ground tied to the saddle of one of the horses with a long rope, started to trot the horses pulling Joe Don behind them, thru the rows of young cotton.. Joe Don was up and running with horse that was pulling him.

His Mother, Janie came running around the house screaming at the men who had Big Abe Green on the back of their truck. Big Abe had been knocked out cold. She saw her son being pulled by the horse. She then ran over to the horse and pulled the rider off of if. She grabbed for the rope tied to her son and screamed, "oh no you don't, you white trash, you let him go, do you hear me, you let him go."

The other horse rider rode over to her and hit her in the back of the head with a police billy-club, it knocked her out and she fell to the ground. The white boy she pulled off of the horse got up from the ground and kicked her in the face three times. He then got back on the horse and told his Dad, "take care of her dad, she wanted to hurt me."

"I'll take care of her, son, don't you worry about that, and I'll take care that the black bitch don't hurt any white people," said the Reverent Shaw of the Club Hill Holinest Baptist Church. He got out of the car of the Grand Wizard Of the Klu Klux Klan of the Mississippi Chapter. He walked out to Janie and hit her again in the back of the head with an axe handle. Janie will be out unconscious for the next dozen hours or so.

Isaiah's other five brothers and sisters were starting to cry and tried to get out from under the house. Isaiah pulled the kids into a circle real close around him and he kept hugging each one to keep them clam. He started quietly singing to them and they started to fall asleep from exhaustion, "Mine eyes has seen the coming of the glory of the lord." Isaiah took off his shirt and pants and put them over the heads of his little brothers and sisters. He would bend to each and sing a new song, "hush little baby don't you cry."

These boys were being put to a test to see if they were man enough or crazy mean enough to join the "KKK". The Reverent told his sons and the other boys, "to get on with the job, these niggers are going to wake up and it's going to come sun up, lets go, get on with it." He then passed the mason jar of homemade corn liqueur to each of the boys and to the Grand Wizard and all took a large drink to build up their courage.

The two boys with Joe Don started to trot their horses again and then they started to race each other. Joe Don kept up with the horse for about a hundred feet then he fell and was dragged about two miles thru the cotton fields and then over the gravel roads. They road back up to the rest of the men pulling what was left of Joe Don, he looked like the flesh had been torn from his body, he was covered with blood, gravel and dirt, he was dead.

The biggest boy jumped off his horse and ran over to the group and laughingly screamed, "Did any of you'al hear that, when that Niggers head hit that big river rock, it sounded like a melon exploding."

All the men started to kind of laugh and dance in a circle and shout and hug each other.

"Drag that black bitch over here, I have a surprise for her," said the Minister. He set down his bible and got a can of the red devil lye that Big Abe used in his cleaning of the metal parts he was working on. *I need to make sure that this bitch can not recognize me, she's cleaned my house many times. God will not let me personally kill some one. But I don't think it's a sin to watch some one get killed.* "Lay her down on her back boys. Boys I did not tell you to take her clothing off, well all right, but take turns and wash you selves after each turn."

The Grand Wizard came walking over undoing the fly to his pants, "Grand Wizard do you want a chance?

Boys move over and let the man in front. Sir it's our pleasure, you go right on a head," said the oldest of the boys. *Damn he's not got much of a Johnson, my little brother has more that him and he's only ten years old.*

"Ok boys, has every body had a turn, Bobby Mac I seen you take two turns, now get out of line." Every body laughed. "Now boys lay that black bitch on her back and hold open her eyes." Said the minister. He pored the red devil lye into Janie's eye, she started to regain her conciseness as it started to burn her eyes out. "Here take this ax handle and knock her silly again," and he poured the red devil lye in her eyes again.

The Grand Wizard finally said, "boys it's time to do the job we came here to do, we've all had a great deal of fun now lets go to work. Bring that truck back over here with that big black buck on the bed. Now remember what I told you on how to tie the end of the rope onto this big tree stump after you throw it over the biggest limb on the oak. Now tie his hands to his sides. Ok boys, one of you drive that truck away and lets watch him swing."

"It's my truck," said Bobby Mac, "I get to drive." The boys started to wrestle as to who was going to drive the truck and hang Big Abe Green.

"Ok boys, it's Bobby Mac's truck, but Bobby Mac you get to drive all the time, let Wilson drive this time," said the Minister.

"Sir, Wilson's crossed eyed, he'll wreck my truck," said Bobby Mac.

"I am not crossed eyed, I'm blind in my right eye from birth," hollered the crossed eyed Wilson Solsby as he climbed into the cab of the truck on the drivers side.

"I'm shot gun," screamed little bucked tooth Robert Lee Hill. As he got into the passengers side of the truck laughing.

"Ah hell, I'll just ride on the hood." said Bobby Mac, mad as hell but resolved to the fact that he was not going to get to drive and hang that upptie, "Nigger". *I'll drive the next one we hang, by god I'll drive, you wait and see.*

Asheville North Carolina

Asheville, North Carolina was a mountain city that all the mountain cities led into. Asheville was considered very progressive and open. The main railroad hub in the mountains of North Carolina, southern Virginia, northern Georgia, and eastern Tennessee was in Asheville as well as the very large round house to turn train engines around. The North Carolina Rail Road company brought money, power, and a sense of affluence to the Western North Carolina and the Eastern Tennessee mountains. After the rail road crossing of the Continental Dived in the eighteen nineties all commerce from logging, to agriculture, and mining for the mineral deposits of the mountains came through Asheville to the railroad yards in Asheville and Biltmore, a small township on the southern side of Asheville. The rail road had passenger stations in all the small towns that the rail road went through. Affluent women took one day trips to shop in the stores and shops in down town Asheville. Salesmen who sold in the Western North Carolina, Northern Georgia, and Eastern Tennessee areas would stay in Asheville in one of the hotels who catered to their needs of gambling, women and alcohol. The head colored gambler called, "Mr. Daddy Rabbit", made sure that these salesmen had plenty of everything to make their stay over night or longer in Asheville a very good one.

Janie Green, was now called "Blind Janie", hugged her now oldest son Isaiah Green, thirteen years old. "Boy you be a good boy, now you hear me. I loved you, Isaiah, your my big boy, now, iffin you don't like that there train, then you just quit and come back home to me."

The young Mr. Isaiah Green and his mother and his brothers and sisters were now living in Asheville, N.C. where his maternal Uncle, George Washington Rudder also resided. Mr. G. W. Rudder was now known as "Mr. Daddy Rabbit". The term of "Mr. Daddy Rabbit" is an earned name in Asheville for the colored head of the family of gamblers, con-men, men who worked prostitutes, fences of stolen items and loan sharks. He had to be a very smart and ruthless man. A man with great charm, but someone that you did not cross in any way. He was known to have committed several murders.

Blind Janie, sister of Mr. Daddy Rabbit, had moved her family away from Mississippi, after the hanging of her husband and the murder of her oldest son. Joe Don, four years ago. Daddy Rabbit [G W Rudder] and two of his body guards took the train to Meridian Mississippi, to gather up his sister and her children after he received the wire of the hanging of Big Abe Green. He vowed revenge for the hanging. He was able to get the name of one of the group who had hung Mr. Abraham Green. He got the name from a neighboring share cropper.

Mr, Daddy Rabbit and one of his body guards found out where Wilson Solsby lived and they waited until they found him feeding the pig he and his father was raining for sale at the county fair. The two North Carolina Colored men waited until Wilson walked to the corn crib for pig food and grabbed him by the neck. Wilson first thought that a couple of his new brothers of the Klu Klux Klan were playing with him, so he did not resist when he was pulled completely behind the barn. When he was let go and he turned to face his friends but saw two very large colored men and he began to pee on him self.

"Who are you boy's, what do you want here? You know coloreds not allowed on white mens farm with out permission, now you boy's let me go and you get out of here. *Who are these niggers, what do they want with me, I'm going to get the Klu Klux Klan to give them a little talking too. Why aint they leavin,* were Wilson Solsbys last thoughts.

John Henry Jenkins, the body guard with Daddy Rabbit, grabbed Wilson and cut his throat with his straight razor. He let the blood pump from Wilsons neck into the pigs pen. This made the very large pig walk over to the new blood and he began to lick up the blood up. Daddy Rabbit began to cut to flesh off of Wilsoms face and feed it to the pig. The two men then let the pig start eating the flesh from Wilsons neck and let the body fall into the pigs pen.

Daddy Rabbit and his body guard rode the two mules back to the colored share croppers farm, when they got to the farm the share cropper said. "Mr. Rabbit," he thought that Daddy Rabbits given name was Rabbit because he kept hearing the body call Daddy Rabbit, "Rabbit," so he called him Mr. Rabbit. "Mr. Rabbit, I'ven got another name for you, Sir, another boy who was with that Preacher that night was his nephew, Robert Lee Hill. He lives over in town behind the cotton exchange."

"Thank you, my good friend, here is a little something you and your family," said Daddy Rabbit as he put two twenty dollar bills into the front shirt pocket of the old share cropper.

"Now my good friend, please have the colored taxi, [a Colored driver with a wagon and a mule pulling it] meet me a Big Abe's place in three hours. And again I thank you."

The old share cropper did not pull out the money that "Mr. Rabbit" put into his until Mr. Rabbit and his friend left. Then the old share cropper pull out the money in his front shirt pocket and found the forty dollars. This was more money than the old share copper had ever had for himself in his whole life. He ran into town to give the message to the colored taxi driver.

Daddy Rabbit and his body guard rode their mules to the back of the cotton exchange, there they asked an old colored gentleman setting on a bale of cotton who Robert Lee Hill was and was he around. The old gentleman pointed to Hill. Daddy Rabbit and Jenkins walked up to Hill and asked if he could show them the front of the warehouse of the exchange. "Sure," said Hill, *I'll show theses two old Niggers around the front for four bits, I have to take my fifteen year old wife out to the high schools talent show ,and I'll have pay her twelve year old ltttle sister a penny to baby sit for us.*

I'll buy the wife and me a soda pop and some boiled peanuts and maybe some cotton candy and I'll still have forty cents

for the fair when it comes next month. These were the sixteen year old, Hills thoughts.

The Cotton Exchange was the largest building in this part of the county. It was a warehouse for the cotton bales to be unloaded by the growers and loading docks for the trains to take the bales to be made into thread for making cloth. It also had an office for the cotton buyers and the exchange owner [one of the richest men the county] and his secretary and bookkeeper. It had a giant scale for weighing the bales of raw cotton. There was a large room for removing the seeds from the cotton and rebaleing it.

Young Robert Lee Hill was the maternal nephew of the owner of the exchange who had gotten the niece of the feed and send stores daughter pregnant when she was barely thirteen. They were second cousins He was given the job as the night watchman to help both families from having to support him and his new family.

Daddy Rabbit and his body guard followed Robert Lee into the warehouse. The body guard hit Robert Lee in the back of the head and knocked his out. Daddy Rabbit had the body guard wrapped Robert Lee in a large canvas sheet and put him across the front of one of the guards mule and the men rode down to the railroad tracks out side of the town about a half mile. The two men set Robert Lee down and revived him. They starting giving him very strong corn liqueur to drink, when he did not want to drink any more, the body guard put his pistol to Robert Lees head and made him drink. When Robert Lee passed out, Daddy Rabbit and the body guard laid Robert Lee on the railroad tracks and place some boiled peanuts, half eaten corn bread and some fried fat back in his pockets. They waited until the freight train came down the tracks and ran over Robert Lee, the town thought he had gotten drunk and was having a picnic on the tracks and had been ran over. He was cut into three parts.

Daddy Rabbit gathered his sister and her remaining children and got on the train in the colored car and headed to Asheville and to the colored hospital there, The Torrence Colored Hospital on Hill Street.

Working On the Rail Road

Daddy Rabbit moved his little sister Janie, into an apartment on Eagle street in the colored section of down town Asheville behind the Asheville police department. The Green family moved into the apartment above the colored stores and little shops, and business offices of Mr. Daddy Rabbit. He then put the children of his sister into the schools for colored children and he gave Janie the job of collecting the money owed Daddy Rabbit by gamblers, the rents owed on properties owned by Mr. Daddy Rabbit, and to be the security for his building. He gave Janie a straight razor and taught her how to you it, how to really hurt someone and just how to scar them up to teach them a lesson, and how too keep it clean and sharp.

Janie Green, now called "Blind Janie" was a fast learner, she could cut someone so fast that they sometimes had to see the blood before they knew that they had been cut. She also knew how to cut someone so that they would be scared up but not dead. Blind Janie could feel coins and tell what domination that they were, she had to have one of her children help her with identifying the paper money.

Blind Janie had to let her oldest son go to work on the Pullman cars on the railroad as a shoe shiner, some one who would shine your shoes while you worn them or you could have your shoes shined at night while you slept and have a shined set of shoes fresh each morning. The shine boy had a small work area in the car that the colored workers slept in. Also in that rail car was an ironing person to have your suit or dress freshly ironed each night. This train ran from New York to Asheville to Charlotte, twice a month to Columbia South Carolina and to Miami then turn around and to have the same stops on the way back to New York. It was a very good job for the colored men. They mostly lived on tips from the passengers. Blind Janies brother was owed so much monies from the manager of the workers on this train that he was able to get Isaiah a job as the shine boy.

Isaiah, in his three years in Asheville had learned how to gamble and how to act as a bookie. After the first round trip on the train he learned who gambled and how and how to act as a bookie for the colored employees. The club car in the back of the train had nickel and penny slot machines and nickel horse racing machines. The colored employees of the train always played these machines in the middle of the night on the trips made from the white passengers while they were cleaning the club car. Isaiah learned how to bet with the colored employees on which machines would pay off. He had learned very well and on his third trip on the train he gave his Mother five dollars he had made that trip. He told her it was for his work as a shine boy. Isaiah worked his way up the working ladder on the train as different colored employees got too old and quit or got to sick to work.

Isaiah looked good, he had red hair and he kept it short and waxed straight back on his head. He had good and straight white teeth. He was about five foot nine inches tall and slender with good skin. The head conductor put him into the dinning car as a waiter because he had very little of a colored accent and he could read and right very well. A lot of the passengers on the trains wanted a well spoken, clean, nice looking waiter to handle their food. Isaiah made three times the tips as a waiter as he did as the shine boy.

He was able to get one of his younger brothers "Little Abraham" the job as a shine boy on his train and he showed him how to do the shine job and how to make good tips and how not to gamble. "Little Abraham" was called just Abraham on the train. He also turned over half of his earnings to his mother on each trip.

Isaiah, also would bring all of the illegal alcohol on the train to resale.

Isaiah started to go to the horse tracks at the Hialeah Race track in Miami, when he was not working on the train as it was being serviced for the trip back up north. He would go to the stables and talk to the stable boys and horse walkers to find out which of the horses were sick or tired or doped up. He learned how to bet with this information. He met a white bookie to place his bets with and he started sharing his information about the horses with this bookie and they became good friends. The bookie was named Ronnie Morris, he was as tall as he was wide, about five foot six inches tall he had his hair combed back in a duck tail. He always wore a panama hat with big flowered shirts and a nice leather sport coat. He loved smoking very big and stinking Cuban cigars.

He, Ronnie Morris, would take Isaiah to the back of "Manseans" restaurant where the Cuban and Colored workers had to eat and he would buy Isaiah the best steak and pasta the restaurant had to offer. Half of the time, Ronnie Morris would join Isaiah and eat with him in the kitchen. Isaiah also learned about wine and which brands and flavors were the best from the Cuban waiters at the restaurant. Isaiah learned a lot about the horse racing business and about the restaurant business hanging around with his friend Ronnie Morris. He was able to meet other white bookies and gamblers thru Ronnie Morris.

In five more years Isaiah was twenty two and he became the head of the waiter staff on the train. He was now the head bookie on the train and he was now taking bets from the white travelers on the train that traveled weekly or monthly as salesman and Isaiah was able to bet with them and he knew who would lose without blaming it on Isaiah and they would pay their loses. Isaiah liked for them to see him with Ronnie Morris in Miami and he would introduce them to the white bookie, so that they would think they were also losing their money to a white man.

Four times a year, when the season was low for the railroads, Isaiah would set up very large poker game on the train from Miami to New York of which Ronnie Morris would be the main player. He would have players from all the stops the train would make. These games were so poplar that Isaiah collected admission fees from gamblers to play. Isaiah would never participate in these games, he sold coffee, beer, wine, water, and cokes. He had the kitchen make sandwiches and soups, and chilies to sell. He also sold cigarette, cigars and women.

The railroad did not object to the gamblers because they bought seats on the train and most of the time they would bring along their lady friends which was another sold seat along with the all the food, beverages, and tobacco products they used, this made money for the railroad There would be as many as fifty seats sold because of the games. The Conductors and all the train personnel made extra money on these trips.

Isaiah also learned to collect pass due debts from the gamblers, train employees or passengers. He found that he was very good at collecting these debts, but he did not like the hard collecting by the hurting of people. There were always off duty policemen in each of the train stops who would help Isaiah collect hard.

He had met an old man who taught him how to carry two knifes to fight with. Isaiah starting carrying a straight razor in his right pants pocket and an old pocket knife in his left pocket. He would pull out his left handed knife first and fumble and drop it to the ground. Most of the time his opponent would bend to pick up the fallen knife. Isaiah would then pull out his straight razor with his right hand and cut his opponent, sometimes to the death. He got very good at this method of protecting him self and he only used this when he felt in danger.

Isaiah loved his job on the train, he was able to spend a couple of days a month with his family in Asheville and he met and had plenty of lady friends who he would meet on the train when they would accompany their employers as there maid or baby setters or health care givers on their trips to or from Miami, Charlotte, Asheville, or New York. Isaiah really liked the "Red Boned" ladies the best. [Red Boned was the term used by colored people for light skinned colored women. White people called these same women, High Yellows.] He was able to entertain these ladies in his birth on the train, being the head waiter and the head of all gambling, he now had the largest single room on the employee car. It was only six feet by four and a half feet, with a pull down single bed, but on a train for employees that was considered very large for a single. Isaiah was also able to show his lady friends a good time with an expensive meal and wine made by the kitchen staff that always owed him money. He had a small Philco radio in his room that would pick up radio stations most of the way back and forth on the trips. Life could not be much better for him.

Isaiah also suffered from night mares from seeing his brother killed and his Father hung and him mother violated and then blinded. He was able to get the names of most of the men who had brutalized and ruined his family and he always swore that he would get even with them. He had the nightmares about that night once or twice a week and he would wake up and pray to meet those red neck men and dream of the actions he would take when he saw one of them.

One day as the train picked up passengers in Columbia South Carolina, which it only did once ever two weeks, An elderly man boarded the train and Isaiah recognized him as the father of two of the boys that killed his brother and lynched his father and this man blinded his mother and had all the other men in the red neck group and the KKK group rape his mother. Isaiah's blood pressure went up so high he thought that he may be having a heart attack. He was so dizzy and he could not think very well that he went into the galley kitchen and walked into the refrigeration unit on the train and cried. The crying and ice cold temperature cleared his head and his thought process.

The evening meal served on the train was a roast beef with all the trimmings and a spaghetti dinner with an Italian meat sauce. The old man came into the dinner car of the train. This train was strictly a passenger train. It could carry over four hundred passengers All the tables in the dinner car was for four, sometimes the passengers would have to share the table with other passengers on the train. The old man had to share his table with a couple with their only child, five year old Robert. Robert ordered the spaghetti dinner with milk, his Father ordered the roast of beef dinner with a glass of unsweeten tea, Roberts Mother asked if she could just have a grilled cheese sandwich with a grape fruit half with a coke. Isaiah had sent one of the other waiters to wait on the old mans table. The old man wanted the roast beef dinner meal, and he told the colored waiter to "hurry up now boy, do you hear me boy?"

When the waiter came in to the kitchen car with the order, Isaiah said he would prepare the roast beef dinner for the old man. Isaiah spit into the gravy he poured over the roast of beef. He looked at Bubba Don and motioned his head up and down which told Bubba Don that he could also do something to the plate of food. Bubba Don put his finger into his nose and pulled out something green and slimy and put it into to the plate of food. Isaiah took the glass of sweeten tea and stuck his Johnson in to it. The whole kitchen staff knew that there was someone in the dinner car who deserved this treatment. They all wanted to see who it was and they wanted to know why.

After the evening meal and the cleaning up of the dinning car and the kitchen, Isaiah told the crew of the reason he wanted this mans food to be nasty. The crew was very upset at what old white man had done to Isaiah's family in Mississippi, they all had relatives that had suffered the same fate in the rural south. The crew asked if they could do more to the old man to get even with him. Isaiah answered, "thank you my friends, let me be the only one that does something to him, I don't want to put your jobs in danger. Baggage clerk, did he bring any luggage on the train with him? Good, take me to it."

In the baggage car Isaiah went through the old red necks luggage he found a wallet with forty five dollars in it. Isaiah new that that was an old trick, a thief would take the forty five dollars and think that they had struck gold. Isaiah keep looking and under the dirty clothing he found wrapped in an old dirty tee shirt he found another larger sum of money. Isaiah took the hidden money of two fifty dollar bills, three twenty dollar bills, six five dollar bills and nine one dollar bills, for a total of two hundred twenty nine dollars. Isaiah went back to the kitchen car and divided the money up between all the dinning and kitchen car staff, this included the shine boy, the ironing boy, the bath cars attendants and clean up boys, and the conductors.

The train crew turned the cars into sleeper cars at bed time and the passengers would sleep until and hour and a half out side of Miami. It was always a mad dash to feed the passengers and turn the sleeper cars back into day cars and get every thing clean in the club car, before the train stopped in Miami.

The kitchen staff made the white red neck that had hurt Isaiah's family a special morning breakfast. They rubbed his toast in the crack of there buttocks, They put his jelly in their mouths before they spit it back in to his individual jelly bowls, and last they rubbed his bacon on their feet after it had cooked.

Even during probation the club car could always serve alcohol drinks. Club cars were always famous and busy because of the alcohol and gambling that started at eight a.m. and closed down at eleven p.m. in the evenings.

Each year this train would get all the new and modern cars and the newest and modern engines. As these new trains were updated the trains would carry more and more passengers. At the end of the great war in the early twenties passenger trains became more and more popular. The American population began to travel more and they wanted to see more of their own country. The train had to hire more employees. Isaiah was able to promote his brother in the shine shop to waiter. He worked with his brother and taught him how to act as a waiter to increase his tips. These tips and regular pay increased his younger brothers pay to double and he now wore a form of a tuxedo. He next hired his another younger brother as the new shine boy. Shine boys now made a lot of money in tips, usually one cent to five cents. Every now and again one of the drunk passengers would toss the shine boy two bits [twenty five cents, a quarter].Isaiah also hired his sister, Lizzie, as the ironing person on the train. The ironing person had a small alcove in which to iron and steam press passengers clothing. This job also worked on tips. The Rail Road company paid most of the employees working on the trains a half a cent an hour, with tips this proved to be a very good job. Isaiah took twenty five percent of his brothers and sister's pay and gave it to Daddy Rabbit to invest it real estate in Asheville for them a home place.

Both boys gave their mother, Blind Janie, five dollars on each round trip of the train and Isaiah also gave her five dollars on each round trip and he also gave his uncle, Mr. Daddy Rabbit, Five dollars a week to purchase property in Asheville. He started buying rooming houses off of Eagle street, in down town Asheville.

The train would stay in Asheville eight hours for cleaning and now for empting the sewer waste into the city sewer that ran into the French Broad River. The clean up crews also washed down the out side of all the train cars. All the trash from the train and kitchen trimmings were separated and each sold to different men for disposal. All the paper trash was burned in the train depot stoves, the clothing thrown away, and there was a lot of it, was sold to a man that ran a used clothing store in the town of Trust, North Carolina. The little store in trust had two women that worked in it that could take used and torn clothing and make it look new and that's how it was sold. The wastes from the bathrooms and kitchens were sold to a farmer who used it as fertilizer for his crops. The rail road employed hundreds of men and also a few women in the Asheville area due to the debts the hiring bosses and supervisors owed "Mr. Daddy Rabbit."

The Growing Up Of Isaiah Green

Isaiah Green traveled down to Key West with his friend Ronnie Morris the bookie on the new railroad line all the way to the last Florida Keys island, Key West. Isaiah and Ronnie Morris gambled and drank the nights away. Isaiah learned to kind of swim, more just a dog paddle. He learned that he liked the kind of life that his friend Ronnie Morris had. Isaiah wanted to buy himself a very large car, but realized that he had no place to keep one. Isaiah made a lot of money by buying illegal alcohol from Cuba and the Bimini Islands and selling it on the trains and to his uncle in Asheville. Isaiah began to make a lot of money and had no real place to spend it. With a depression going on, Isaiah was able to let his uncle loan out his money at very high interest rates.

Mr. Daddy Rabbit told Isaiah that they needed to buy a building, each to own half, and that Daddy Rabbit needed to run his gambling from. They found a two story building on Southside Avenue, it was four thousand square feet on the main floor and the same on the second floor. It also had a very old boarding house that had fallen into disrepair on the property. It was in too bad of shape to be fixed so they had it torn down .and graveled it for a parking lot. The second floor was a storage area for all the supplies that Daddy Rabbit had in his bootlegged bar business and his gambling business. Isaiah built his apartment on the roof and that made the building three stories. Isaiah stayed in his apartment when he was not staying on the train and it was a place for him to entertain the ladies that he went out with and a place for him to be alone to think and rest..

Daddy Rabbits son, George Washington Rudder Junior, also built an apartment on the third floor. G W Junior helped run the every day business's for Daddy Rabbit. G W Junior was bring groomed to take over the "Daddy Rabbit" position in the family when the present Daddy Rabbit retired, just quit, or was killed.

G W Rudder Junior, and Isaiah Green were very close friends and first cousins. They shared all their ideas, thoughts, and plans with each other. Their future plan for Asheville and the surrounding area was to divide it into two equal parts. Isaiah was going to have all the gambling an illegal booze for the town of Asheville.

Isaiah again began to float into a very good life, his family was doing good and he was doing great. He was making lots of money and seeing a lot of women. He loved his life, he loved his siblings, and he loved his job. He felt that his life could not get much better.

On his next trip he got his train employees ready for a breakfast meal pulling out of Columbia, South Carolina, he again saw the old red neck that hurt his family. His kitchen crew also saw the old man, they winked at each other and nodded their heads and smiled at Isaiah, he smiled back. His wait staff and the kitchen staff really fixed the old mans breakfast, his lunch, and his evening mean. The old man was up most of the night sick and throwing up. He was so sick that he decided to miss the morning breakfast on the train out side of Miami.

The old man got off the train and called a taxi to take him to a hotel on the Miami Beach strip across the Indian River. Isaiah also had a colored taxi take him to the back entrance of the same hotel where all colored and Cubans were allowed to enter. Isaiah crossed the lobby of the hotel and he gave the half asleep bell boy a fin [a five dollar bill] and took his bell cap. Isaiah then went to the old man and said, "I'll carry your bags to your room sir," and then he got onto the elevator with the old mans luggage.

The old man told the elevator operator, "number 413." When the elevator stopped at floor four, the old man walked off the elevator toward his room without tipping the elevator operator. Isaiah fallowed him to room 413 and then he carried the old mans luggage into the room. The old man gave Isaiah a penny as a tip. Isaiah then kicked the old man behind the knees and the old man fell to the floor, he looked up and saw Isaiah and screamed, "Pick me up, boy, boy I said now!" The old man thought that he had fallen, he did not know that Isaiah had kicked him behind the knees. "Boy, I said for you to pick me up, do you hear me Nigger, I said for you to pick me up, before I call your boss man, now get your black ass over here, boy."

"Yes Boss," was Isaiahs reply, "I'm right hear Boss, let me help you into this chair."

You better boy, do you hear me, boy, hear I'll give you another brownie [slang for a penny]. Now pour me some water, boy, did you hear me boy," was what the old man said to Isaiah.

Isaiah pulled out his straight razor and said to the old man, "sir, do you recognize me, I'm from Meridian Mississippi, your from there too aren't you. You and your boys hung my father, Big Abe Green, you also killed my brother, Joe Don Green, and you all raped and blinded my mother, Janie Green. Do you remember us now you old Bastard."

"I don't know what your talking about boy, now get out of my room before I call the hotel Manager. He'll fire an uppity Nigger like you. Now you get out of my room before I call for help, and I said now, do you hear me, boy." The old man could not remember hanging a Big Abe, from Meriden Mississippi, he was evolved in so many lynching's. He smiled when he tried to remember one of the colored girls he had raped, he did like the dark girls and he did like to abuse them, but he was getting old and there was so many of them, he could not remember just one. "Now did you hear me boy?" This old man had never been treated like this by a darkie, he was kind of surprised. *What's this, why is my neck and shoulder wet, is this blood, is this my blood, did that nigger cut me, I'll have him hu.* Those were his last thoughts as he slid into death. Isaiah had cut his throat and watched him die.

"Now old man, you go to hell," said Isaiah out load. Isaiah was surprised that he felt nothing. This was the first man he had killed, he thought that he would fill remorse or sad, or even happy, he felt nothing. He had to get back to the train.

He picked up a serving tray and put a water picture on it with two glasses. He put a hand towel over his arm, He walked out of the room and went to the service stairs in the hotel. He still had on the bell boys' hat so no body even paid him any attention, bell boys were all over the hotel serving the guest. Isaiah walked into the hallway that leads into the back street. He put down the tray and it's contents, and threw the hat away as he stepped into the large ally and walked to the opening and hailed a colored cab. That evening he met his friend Ronnie Morris and told him the story of the lynching of his father, and why he had to kill the old white red neck and how he had killed him.

"I'm taking you out for the best steak in town, I'm taking you to the Florida Hotel on the Miami Beach. I'll get us a room and have room service serve us.They have the best steak and lobster tails with all the trimmings, there are. We'll eat and drink a good wine and just relax.

You need to get all that out of you system. It had to be done my friend, It had to be done." Said Ronnie Morris as he hugged Isaiah, "It had to be done, my old friend."

For the next week, Isaiah wasn't sure how he really felt, was he happy or sad. Was he regretting that he had to take a mans life? He decided that he was fine with his feelings with the events, that the old bastard needed to die, painfully. On his next trip to Asheville, Isaiah told his mother all about the event.

How it made him feel.

"My son, I'm proud of the man you have become, you're a good son, you're a good brother, and a very good man.

I want you to try to forget about all that stuff that happened to us in Mississippi, don't let all that stuff haunt you and make you a bad person. Live your life for all that's new for you out there, for all the new adventures there is for you to live, for all the new and good people your going to meet," said Blind Janie as she hugged and kissed him.

Cuba and Mexico

Everything had settled back down in Isaiah's life, he worked and he found out that work was very good therapy for him. He found that when working he was able to go back into his mind and forget about the past. On his next trip to Miami he called Ronnie Morris the next morning and said, "Ronnie, do you still want me to go to Cuba with you on a little vacation?"

Ronnie Morris, screamed, "hell yes, I always wanted to show you Cuba, now I'm always packed for Cuba, I'll meet you at the fishing boat docks at Dinner Key. Look for the boat named ' Miss. 29th Street', I know the owner and he'll take us there for a couple of quarts of good rum and a box of Cuban cigars. Now don't be late, I would hate to get to Cuba with all the women and food there and leave you behind"

"I'll be there partner, you'll see me, I'll be the skinny colored man dressed just like you, except that my panama hat will be wider and taller that yours," laughed Isaiah, and he hung up the phone and ran and started getting ready by putting on his Florida Keys saddles, his new linen white slacks, his bright flowered Carrabin shirt, his big Cuban cigar, and then he put his wide brimmed Panama hat on, and he packed his luggage. And now he was ready for his new adventure with his pal Ronnie in Cuba. As he left the train, he told his brothers and sister, who also worked on the train where he was going and with who. Both of his siblings had meet Ronnie Morris and knew all about him.

Ronnie Morris had been to Cuba many times. He knew where all the bars, bordellos, and gambling houses were located. He had been to them all and lost a lot of money in each of them, but would swear that he always had a good time and they were always glad to see him. He saw Isaiah at the dock at Diner Key and started waving to him, He hugged Isaiah and said, "good to see you my best friend, now how long can we stay in Cuba?"

"I've got four days and three nights off before I have to board my train., so lets party, get drunk, whore around a little, and gamble, I'm ready to blow off some steam." Said Isaiah as he shook the hand of Ronnie Morris and hugged him back. In Cuba, the men climbed into a cab and headed for a hotel with a casino and plenty of alcoholic drinks, floor shows with half naked women, and prostitutes.

"Come on, I'm going to show you a new game in Cuba that's very famous here, it's call Hi Lai. It's a very fast game and there's plenty of betting. Here's you a little paper that describes how the game is played and how you can bet, study up on this, it maybe very easy to lose your money," said Morris. He knew about losing to Hi Lai because he was cleaned out twice at this game. He first time he lost, he had to sell his cloths and shoes to get boat fare back to Miami. The second time he lost he had to talk a fisherman who left Havana and docked in Miami to sell his fish every other day into to letting him ride on the fishing boat to Miami. He had to gut and clean fish on the twelve hour ride as his fare on the fishing trip to the Diner Key Marina. He was covered with fish guts and smells. Ronnie Morris wanted to teach his best friend, Isaiah Green, how to bet on Hi Lai, but he was not sure that he knew how to place bets himself. He did not want to look stupid in his knowledge of Hi Lai to Isaiah, so he had to find a way to teach Isaiah the rules of the game, without losing all of his own and Isaiah's money. He decided to hire a couple of the Cuban prostitutes that hung around one of the Hi Lai arenas. At the Hi Lai games, Isaiah met an elderly Jewish gentleman who owner a large bar and gambling house in Miami.

CHAPTER 5

Miami

The men took a boat to Miami. Franz had four large suitcases, two suit bags, and six shoeboxes. Isaiah had only one ragged, medium-sized suitcase.

Isaiah met with his new partner in the bar and bookie joint. He took the keys and gave Franz a copy. The men had to find a place where they both could live. Miami was like the rest of the south—coloreds did not mix with whites—so they had to find a place where they could live together without any trouble.

They found a place in downtown Miami. Franz told the landlord that Isaiah was his butler and housekeeper. Franz knew that Isaiah had very few clothes and they were cheap, and he had only two pairs of shoes while Franz had seven.

Franz measured Isaiah and went shopping. He bought Isaiah two tuxes, two pairs of patent-leather shoes, sandals, a pair of black wingtips, and a white suit and a dark-blue suit. He also bought a dozen white shirts and a dozen ties. Franz had Isaiah try on the clothes, and he pinned them to fit. He took them to a seamstress and had them tailored.

Franz showed Isaiah how to dress and act like a successful gentleman. The two became almost twins. Isaiah liked his new style and looks and really liked Franz. He was thankful every day that he had met Franz and that he had not cut him when Franz had spilled that drink on him. They became as close as brothers.

Isaiah started buying beer from Jamaica, which was much better than the local bootlegged beers. He bought Canadian whiskey that came through Jamaica. His club had the reputation of having the best booze and the best odds at gambling. Business was going well.

The pair made good business partners. Any money lost gambling from white Miamians had to be collected by Franz, who could go into white neighborhoods and white businesses to collect. Franz had the reputation of not being afraid to go into the colored section of town to collect either.

Business was going so well that Franz had to hire a driver who would also be a bodyguard. He hired a man his neighbor had told him about, the father of a neighbor's wife. Franz told the neighbor to have the gentleman come to his house at noon and take the guys to work. At noon, there was a knock at the door. Isaiah opened the door, and Franz could hear an exchange of words and a laugh.

Isaiah came into the kitchen. "You're not going to believe this. Our bodyguard and driver is here to take us to work." He laughed again.

Franz went into the living room and saw an old gentleman. He looked eighty. He was about six seven and maybe a hundred and fifty pounds of skinny. He was white haired and dressed in black suit, tie, shirt, shoes, and socks. He had an army Colt .45 automatic in a shoulder holster under his coat. His glasses were so thick that they looked like the bottoms of Coke bottles. When Franz introduced himself and shook the gentleman's hand, he noticed the man's hands were arthritic. *How could this very old man ever draw and hold that gun?* "I'm Franz Charles, and this is Mr. Isaiah Green."

CHAPTER 6
Doyle

"I'm Doyle. My granddaughter said I was your new driver."

Isaiah laughed. Franz thought, *Grandfather? I thought I was hiring the father! What am I going to do about this? I can't fire him. I'm trying to get along with my neighbors. I'll let him work a few days then tell him I no longer need a driver. Yeah, that'll work.* "Mr. Doyle, how well do you know Miami, especially downtown?" Franz asked.

"Been here about forty years. I know every street here and in Miami Beach. Please just call me Doyle."

"It's time for work," Isaiah said. "Let's get going."

Doyle went out first and opened the doors to the car for the men. Franz noticed that Doyle had a box with him. "What's in the box?" Franz asked.

"It's my lunch. My wife, Bea, packed it for me. I have to watch what I eat. My doctor has me on a pretty strict diet."

Isaiah, who was giggling in the backseat, elbowed Franz.

They had to make a dozen stops on the way to work to pick up money they were owed, pick up some rum at the docks that had been smuggled in from Cuba, and pick up their dry cleaning and laundry. Their last stop was at a Chinese restaurant to pick up dinner. Franz asked Doyle, "You want any Chinese food?"

"No sir. That's too spicy for me, and I don't eat foreigners' food anyway. I just eat plain old American food."

Again, Isaiah giggled. Franz showed Doyle where to park, and then he showed him all around the bar and the backrooms where the gambling went on.

Doyle asked, "Where do you want me to be while we're here?"

Franz pointed out a raised booth in the corner between the bar and the gaming tables. It had a chair, a shotgun, a nice fan, and a telephone. Doyle hung his black fedora on a nail and sat to watch over the gambling.

Again, Isaiah giggled and punched Franz in the side. Franz was trying his best to hold back his own laughter. Isaiah asked Franz, "Explain this to me. If there's any trouble, do we wake Doyle up or let him sleep right through it? And if we wake him up real fast, is he going to jump up with that shotgun and kill us all because he can't see us?"

"Are you sure he's asleep? He might be dead." Franz said, and both men roared with laughter.

Around ten that evening, Doyle got up, grabbed a newspaper, and asked Franz, "Where's the can?"

Franz pointed to a green door with a "Men" sign.

About fifteen minutes later, Isaiah came up to Franz. "Light a match. There's something dead in the men's room."

Franz shook his head. "It was just Doyle."

"Jesus! What the hell is he eating? Damn, that's bad."

But over the next few months, Dole became very valuable to Franz and Isaiah. He was a great source of knowledge of people, he helped Isaiah invite new gamblers to the club, and he told Isaiah who would pay and who would skip out and where they would be hiding. He knew who had just hijacked a truck and where to buy the goods they had hijacked.

Franz and Isaiah now had five tuxes and five other suits apiece. They also had shirts, jackets, underwear, and shoes, all stolen. Franz had them tailored to fit Isaiah and himself. They had nice leather furniture, radios, record players, and watches all from hijackers.

Doyle also knew the jockeys and horse trainers at Hialeah, and he knew the dog track handlers, good men to know if you were a gambler, and Isaiah and Franz were certainly that.

Bea, Doyle's wife, always sent in pies, cookies, and cakes for the guys. She was a great dessert chef. Franz got a chance to meet her. She had to be close to seventy. She was short and round with rosy red cheeks and her hair in a bun. She and Doyle made quite a pair.

Bea asked Franz which church he attended. He told her a colored church. He knew she would not ask him any more questions about church. Franz had not been to church sense he was thirteen. He refused to go after the minister at his parents' church had slapped him in the face during a service. Franz did not think what he was doing warranted a slap in public. All he did was cup his hand in his armpit under his shirt and make a gassy noise every time the minister took a step by squeezing his arm on his hand. Most people at the service had found that amusing, but the minister had come over and slapped Franz.

His dad took him home and told him he did not have to go back to that church ever again. Franz knew his Dad did not like the minister touching his son but knew that at a church college, the staff had to attend church.

That night at evening service, Herbert told his friends, "Franz is the way he is because of all the bug bites he received as a little boy living out in the forest as he had to for three years. The bites must have been poison. It has to be something like that, right? Children are just not that bad, are they?"

Business was doing well. Franz and Isaiah were living like kings. They had money to buy a boat, and they had plenty of women, travel, and good times. Isaiah and Franz were very successful Miami businessmen who hung out with a group of businessmen, not all of whom were honest, but they all had money and enjoyed good times. Sundays were for the horse or the dog tracks, the other season was for jai alai, the game they had seen in Cuba, which they learned was just as popular in Miami.

In 1929, the Great Depression hit the country. Banks failed, and many people lost all their money. This happened to Franz and Isaiah when their bank closed. The half-dozen banks that the bookies, bootleggers, and gamblers used crashed the same as all the rest. The bankers who had lost all the money left town that morning or they would have been hacked up and put into the bay.

It took a couple of months before the bar was making any money again, and gamblers were scarce. Isaiah's bar was in the poorest part of town, and it took a while for it to come back alive, but it was not like it had been.

One night about two in the morning, two men, a Cuban and an American, jumped Isaiah in the parking lot of the bar. They did not see Franz walk up on them. As soon as they turned to see who it was, he shot both in the head.

"Damn, that was loud!" Isaiah said. "Thanks, man. What do we do with the bodies?"

Doyle came around the building running as fast as he could, which was rather slow. He was trying to pull his gun but could not get it out of its holster.

"You don't need that now, Doyle," Franz said. "But do you have any ideas on what we can do with the bodies?"

"Yeah, I have an idea. Let's load them up in their car."

The boys loaded the two holdup men into their car, and Isaiah drove behind Doyle in their new black Oldsmobile. They went out in the everglades. Doyle had them stop. He asked Franz if he could borrow his knife. Franz gave it to him. Doyle slit the throats of the two dead men and pushed them into the water.

"Man, you didn't need to do that," Isaiah said. "They're already dead."

"I know," said Doyle. "This will help call the gators to dinner."

Just then, a large alligator grabbed one of the men and took him underwater.

Doyle said, "The other one won't last long either. Let's go."

On the way back to Miami, the men stopped at an all-nighter and had coffee and donuts. Isaiah asked Doyle, "How did you know to do that?"

"I was a cop for forty years," Doyle said, "twenty in New York and twenty here. I've seen it all and done most of it."

"Don't you want to retire?" asked Isaiah.

"I was retired for ten years. There's only so much fishing you can do. My grandkids are too old to play with, I'm too old to run the women anymore, and all my friends died years ago. I like being with you boys. You know how to live life and have a good time."

Because times were tough in the bar and gambling business, Franz had to hire himself out to other gamblers as their collector to keep the money rolling in. Isaiah had to start selling his good whiskey and beer to the hotels in Miami Beach and serve his customers the cheaper, locally made beers and whiskey to stay afloat. While Isaiah was at a large hotel on Indian River, he noticed the kitchen staff was throwing away a lot of rolls and bread and raw vegetables, cold cuts, and pastries. Isaiah asked the kitchen supervisor why it was all being thrown away.

"It was from this morning's breakfast and brunch. We're not allowed to refrigerate it again and serve it tomorrow."

"Can I buy it from you?" asked Isaiah.

"No," said the supervisor, "that's against our policy."

"Okay," said Isaiah. "Will you trade for it?"

"That also may be against the hotel policy, but if we can work something out, what would you do with all this food?"

"I'd give it to the families of my customers. My bar is in the poorest section of Miami. Those people have nothing and cannot afford to buy anything. How about if I trade you a bottle of good, bonded, double-malt scotch?"

"Yes, but you have to keep this deal quiet," said the supervisor.

They shook hands on the deal. Isaiah would trade the scotch for food about three times a week. Isaiah told his bartenders to serve the food to the regular paying customers and let their wives come in for a couple of sandwiches to take home. That applied to the regular gamblers also. Isaiah figured he could keep people in his bar and help their families. Times were tough, and everyone needed to help; Isaiah wanted his gamblers to keep coming in. Bea would bring in oranges, tomatoes, and avocados she grew in her yard.

The bar started to make money again, not a lot, but enough to keep the doors open. Isaiah's partner, the elderly Jewish man, liked Isaiah's ideas, especially those that allowed him to stay in business. Franz was home only about two days a week. He was having to travel all over

Florida to make a living—collecting for bookies—but even that was getting difficult.

One day when Franz was in Pensacola, he decided to rejoin the military. He thought he would try the navy, this time to be an Officer or a pilot. He went to the Pensacola Naval Air Station and tried to join up. The recruiter checked his record and told him the navy was not interested because Franz had never graduated high school. Franz tried the army and was told the same. As he was closing the door to the army recruiter's office, he overheard the Sergeant saying, "Lock the door. We don't want that man back in the service ever!"

In 1932, some states began to pass state laws that allowed the manufacture of alcoholic spirits, so some of the tourist area such as Miami Beach began to openly serve alcoholic drinks, beer, and wine. The nation was tired of the Volstead Act.

In April 1933, 3.2 beer became legal again, and soon after that, the Volstead Act was repealed. That almost put little bars like Isaiah's out of business. It seemed everybody in South Florida went into the bar business, and it was cheaper to buy alcohol and take it home to drink. Isaiah and Franz became small-time hustlers who made a living selling stolen property from hijacked trucks, untaxed cigarettes from North Carolina, and untaxed rum from Cuba. Franz and Isaiah would take their boat to Cuba for cigars and to Bimini for rum. The boys had to work hard, much harder than they wanted to work; they no longer had the time to dress nice and go out on the town. Doyle would go on each of these boat trips with the boys, and he usually slept the whole time on the water. He never took his hat or coat off. He would just sit in a deck chair and snore loudly.

One day early in 1935, the boys were in the backseat, Doyle driving. He pulled up to a red light. They stayed stopped after the light changed. The cars behind them were blowing their horns. Franz bent to the front of the car to tell Doyle to move on, but he looked like he was asleep. Franz touched Doyle's hand and realized Doyle had passed away.

Franz and Isaiah were two of the pallbearers. At the family reception, Bea told the guys that Doyle had thought of them as his sons, that he had always talked about them. He had his most fun being with them. Franz asked the granddaughter if Bea was going to be okay and if she had any money to live on. Doyle's granddaughter told Franz that Doyle had never trusted the banks; he had kept his money in silver and gold coins in safety deposit boxes at three banks. Doyle had left Bea very well off. She had more money than she would ever spend.

The granddaughter gave Doyle's .45 Colt to Franz and his old service revolver to Isaiah. Both men cherished their gifts.

A couple of months later, Isaiah's mother called to tell him that the family patriarch was dying and that he needed to come home to become the new family patriarch. His mom wanted to be the head of the family, but they told her she was too old and blind as well. Her name was Blind Janie. She ran a cleaning service and an illegal bar, liquor by the drink. Buying any alcohol on Sundays was against the law in North Carolina, so Blind Janie's was always busy.

Blind Janie's cleaning service ran like this. If you wanted to hire a colored maid or cook or housekeeper in Asheville, you had to hire them through Blind Janie. She charged the colored women ten cents a week to work for white families. She had a reputation of cutting nonpayers with a straight razor.

Though the Charles family did not pay either one of their colored women any money, Brigitta Charles still had to pay Blind Janie her ten cents a week for each woman. Blind Janie also owned a couple of boarding houses off Eagle Street. She was considered one of the riches women in Asheville and probably the meanest.

She was so disappointed she was not allowed to be head of the family, but she loved her son and knew he would be a good and fair leader. He would take over an illegal bar, a gambling joint, and a very lucrative bookie business. He would also get a piece of all business done on his property. Isaiah had trained for the job all his life. He had learned to run nightclubs, bookie joints, and gambling houses. He had learned to be ruthless and trust no one except Franz, in whom he had total trust. Isaiah felt that Franz completed him, that they were bookends.

Isaiah had learned to be a gentleman and act and dress as an educated man from Franz. Isaiah would no longer be called Isaiah Green but Daddy Rabbit, the fifth Daddy Rabbit. His uncle had been

Daddy Rabbit for twenty years. Daddy Rabbit told Franz that he had to leave Miami and return to Asheville to take over the family business.

"Let's ride up there together," Franz said. "I'll go to Mars Hill and see my family. Who knows? I might be able to find a job at the college."

"Doing what?" asked Daddy Rabbit.

"I could be in charge of the financial office or coach football."

"You coach football? All you'd do is fix the scores to win bets," Daddy said with a laugh.

"Damn right," said Franz, laughing too. "Actually, Isaiah—no, now I'll you Daddy. Actually, Daddy, I've not seen family in fifteen years. It's about time."

Isaiah sold all their furniture, and Franz sold the boat. The guys went to see Bea and tell everyone good-bye.

CHAPTER 7
Asheville

The trip took two days. Daddy dropped Franz at the rail yard in Asheville and headed to Blind Janie's.

In the station office, Franz hugged Otto. To his surprise, he was really glad to see him and feel part of a family again. Otto told Franz to stay in Asheville with him and Brigitta for a couple of days. They would take him to see his parents that weekend, and then he could stay with them a while in Mars Hill.

"Besides, you need to meet all my children."

"How many do you have?" asked Franz.

"Six," said Otto.

"Six? Jesus."

"There's Leslie. He's seventeen and in college. Then there's Albert, thirteen, and John Henry, eleven, Ava, ten, Sonja, nine, and then the baby, Herbert, six. They're good kids. You'll love them."

Franz agreed. He went home with Otto. Franz was impressed with Otto's home and the kids. He could tell that Brigitta called all the shots in the family. Otto had a large home with two maids. They had two cars. Franz thought, *This is the kind of family you always read about in the magazines. They're happy and successful even in times as bad as these. The world should copy my big brother.*

Otto and his family took Franz to Mars Hill to see the rest of the family. Herbert was a successful music teacher. Stella was the head dietician at the women's dorm. John, his third brother, was an engineer supervisor with the Civilian Conservation Corps on a New Deal project called the Blue Ridge Parkway. Etta, his sister, was a schoolteacher, and Otto, his big brother, was the supervisor of telegraph and teletype operations at the rail yard in Asheville. Franz thought, *I need to succeed now. I have to be equal to or better than my family. I don't want to embarrass them.*

Herbert was glad to see his son, whom he thought had certainly grown up to be a well-dressed, polished, good-looking man.

Everyone asked Franz what he had been doing all these years. He told them he had been in the import and export business. Otto asked him why he was moving back to North Carolina. Franz told him that the big import and export companies in New York were running all the little guys like him out of business. Otto and the family believed him. Franz had always been able to tell a good story. At times, he believed them himself. The story worked because Franz was so polished and well spoken. He had the vocabulary of a college man and dressed like a New York banker.

When Franz was in New Orleans, he met a young woman studying for a PhD in modern European history from Louisiana State. Both of her parents were professors at the university; her father taught medieval European history and her mother taught Scandinavian history. Franz had met her at a dentist's office in Baton Rouge. She was there for a cleaning while Franz was there getting free dental work from the horse-betting dentist.

They became an item right away. Franz moved in with her. She noticed his reading and writing skills were bad. She decided he would have to educate himself. Miss Alice Mauney had a set of encyclopedias and taught Franz to read and understand what he read in them. She also taught him penmanship. After two years, he could read with the best of them and write eloquently. And he liked hanging around the college-professor crowd.

One day when Franz got home from collecting, he noticed his clothes were packed. He asked Alice, "What's going on? I thought we had a good thing going. Where am I moving to?"

"Professor Roberts called to tell us his wife had died on a dig in Scotland a couple of months ago. He's always been the love of my life, and now he says he needs me to come to Scotland with him. I'm going."

"Am I coming with you?"

"No. I'm in love with him," she barked.

Franz was surprised about the move, but he always knew he and Alice were not in love. He had learned a lot from her and would always appreciate her for it.

CHAPTER 8
Mars Hill College

Franz moved into a small student apartment next to campus. He walked the campus daily on his way to breakfast at diners downtown. He bought a new convertible, and he loved riding around campus and stopping to talk to coeds. He would sometimes talk to professors, and they all figured him to be a college man. He loved to talk about ancient history.

He was beginning to run out of money, so he started looking for work. Stella got him a job as a cook at the main dining hall on campus, but that was not for Franz. He was a great chef, not a lunchroom cook. He took a job as a clerk at a drug store, but stocking shelves and sweeping up was not for him either.

He was lost when it came to working in a small town like Mars Hill, which had no nightclubs or bars. The whole town shut down at five thirty every evening. All the people went home. Franz would drive to Asheville for beer, wine, and cigarettes he sold out of the trunk of his car to students. He started going to games on campus and became the local bookie. He started to date some coeds. Rumors started around town about him being a ladies' man. The students knew Franz was the go-to guy if they needed to borrow money or buy anything not allowed on campus. Rumors started going around that Franz was seeing some of the town's married women.

Late one evening, the panel truck owned by the sheriff of Madison County was robbed on the Marshall Highway as it hauled beer, wine, and liquor to the sheriff's office at the courthouse in Marshall. The sheriff was the main bootlegger in the area. The thief took a couple hundred dollars, a case of whiskey, and two cases of beer. The sheriff sent out a posse to comb the area for his money and booze. Nothing was found.

Two months later, the truck was robbed on its way to Asheville to pick up a load of alcohol. That time, the thief got away with five hundred dollars. The sheriff was at that point very upset. He offered a big reward for anyone to turn in anyone involved.

Franz was feeling good about himself. He was making good money again and having a good time. He was doing what he liked best—hustling. He had to physically remind a few people that they had to pay him money they owed him because of loans or bets, and he liked that too. Franz had to take musical instruments, radios, jewelry, or at times cars as payment, but he always got his money. He filled up the pawn shops in the area with most items, but he kept the nice jewelry.

Franz found out he could buy college term papers for almost nothing and resell them to students for good money. Franz also found a way to blackmail the city officials, politicians, department heads, and professors who cheated on their spouses. He even helped set some of those people up.

He held up the sheriff's booze truck again. That time, the sheriff knew who had done it. The sheriff and two deputies headed to Mars Hill to arrest Franz. They planned to kill him when he escaped from jail. One deputy, who was in debt to Franz, called to warn him.

Franz knew he had no way of escaping. He called Daddy Rabbit, Otto, the chancellor of the college, the mayors of Marshall and Mars Hill, and the minister of a large Baptist church in the area who was also head of the Ku Klux Klan there. He drove with Herbert, his dad, to the sheriff's office in Marshall. Each of the men Franz had called came to the sheriff and asked if they could bail Franz out or at least pay his fine. The sheriff knew that with all these people wanting to help Franz, there was no way he could kill him. And the sheriff really wanted to kill Franz. The sheriff agreed to let Franz go if he left Madison County and guaranteed to never come back. He was not to go to Mars Hill to pack. He was to leave right then.

"I'll take him right now," Daddy Rabbit said. "Get in the car, Franz. We're leaving."

Franz hugged his dad and said good-bye. He and Daddy Rabbit drove away.

"Thanks," said Franz. "That was close."

"What the hell kind of mess did you get yourself into?" Daddy asked.

So on the drive to Asheville, Franz told Daddy all about his stay in Mars Hill and how he had made his living. He told Daddy to take him to Otto's house and he would call Daddy the next day. Daddy agreed.

Franz had to tell Otto the whole story of his life in Mars Hill, which made Otto wonder, *How could one man get in so much trouble in such a short time in a small, sleepy, church-college town like Mars Hill?*

Herbert had already called Otto and asked if Franz could live with him. He said that when Otto and Brigitta's children were ready for college, Herbert would arrange for them to go to Mars Hill for free and they could live with him and Stella.

Brigitta gave Franz the choice of staying in one of the children's room or in the basement in a private room with a bath he would share with the colored help. Franz liked being near the ironing room so he could iron his clothes every day. He agreed to cook at least one meal a week.

Herbert and Stella showed up the next morning with all of Franz's belongings, including his convertible. Herbert and Otto had a long talk about Franz. "Otto, Franz always looked up to you. While he was growing up, he seemed to listen to you more than anyone else. Try to help him find himself and become a good, decent man. You know he fell a lot out in the woods you all had to live in for a few years. I'm sure he hit his head so many times that he did some brain damage to himself. That has to be why he acts the way he does."

Brigitta told Franz he would have to pay two dollars a week for his room and board. Leslie, her oldest child, was going to work at the navy shipyard in Norfolk, Virginia, for the summer, and she needed the extra money.

Franz agreed. He knew that was a good deal. He promised himself that whatever he did, he would not bring any harm to the family. If he had to get into the same kind of business he seemed to do best at, he would make sure to keep Otto's family out of it.

CHAPTER 9
Daddy Rabbit

Franz called Daddy Rabbit and told him to pick him up at the railroad depot office because he was going to work with his brother and he wanted to talk to Daddy.

At lunchtime, Daddy drove up and shook hands with Otto. As Daddy and Franz were leaving, Daddy said to Otto, "I need to talk to your brother about a job. I'll bring him home later if that's okay."

"Sure," said Otto. He thought, *What kind of work does this Mr. Rabbit do? What does he wants Franz to do? Maybe he's in the restaurant business and wants Franz to cook. It has to be something good. He dresses like a million bucks.*

Franz and Daddy drove to Daddy's nightclub and gambling establishment. Daddy laid out the whole operation for Franz. "I need you to work with me again. You're the only person in this world I trust."

"You're doing well! What do you need me for?" asked Franz.

"Same thing, man. I need someone of class who can handle himself and who is fearless. Someone who can go into the white neighborhoods and businesses to collect. Those white men owe me a fortune, but I can't collect. You collect with interest, and you keep the interest and fines you put on them. Just remember we want them to come back in to gamble," said Daddy.

"If you're sure you really need me, I'm your man. When do I start?"

"Tonight. I want you to collect hard so the gamblers will know there's a new collector in town. Tonight, I'll show you the operation and introduce you to my employees. I think a couple of them are stealing from me. I want you to find out and take care of them for me. My mom, Blind Janie, runs a couple of prostitutes out of my club, and that's okay. I just don't want the women rolling any drunks. Take care of them also. Your new job title will be chief of security. You do your job your way. You don't have to ask me or tell me anything. I want you to know that I completely trust you."

"Thanks, Daddy, I appreciate that. Don't worry. I'll take care of your business."

The men shook hands and hugged.

The first night on the job, Franz caught one of the dealers cheating. The man was palming cards and making sure his partner at the table was winning. Franz waited until closing to have the bouncers grab the dealer and his partner. Franz took all their money. The dealer had only eleven dollars on him, but his partner had about three hundred and fifty. Franz took the dealer to the door and put his dealing hand on the doorjamb. He slammed the door on the man's hand three times to be sure he had broken it. He grabbed the partner's hand and did the same.

Half of the employees and some customers were still in the bar. It did not take but a couple of days before all the employees and patrons of the club and gambling tables to get the word that this white boy was crazy and extremely mean and that they better not let him catch them doing anything wrong.

Franz and Daddy dressed alike—black tuxes, white shirts with black bow ties, and highly polished black shoes. Their hair was combed straight back. The women thought this white man was the best-looking gangster they had ever seen.

The country was recovering from the Depression. All the government work programs had been successful, and the taxes the government received on alcoholic beverages were helping. People went out more; they seemed to have spending money again. Daddy's nightclub and his gambling house were doing well, especially sense Franz was the collector. Franz would track down those who owed Daddy money and collect it as well as the fee Franz charged.

One day, Franz went into a café and asked the owner for the money he owed Daddy. The man told Franz to get lost. He told him that money lost to a colored man did not really have to be paid back. "Now get the hell out of my café!" he screamed. The man's wife was behind the counter collecting from the patrons for their meals. Franz walked over to her, grabbed her hand, and broke her finger in front of the diners and the owner. Franz took the money she was counting, about four dollars, and told her he would be back the next day to collect the rest or break another one of her fingers. He would break one a day until they paid all they owed. He told them if that didn't work, he would start breaking their children's fingers.

They paid Daddy the money the next day, eighty-five dollars.

Franz had to go to Mrs. Johnson's grocery store on Haywood Road to collect money from the butcher, Mr. O'Kelly. Mr. O'Kelly picked up his meat cleaver and told Franz, "Get out of this store!"

Franz picked up a gallon can of lard and smacked the butcher on his head. When the man got up, his head was bleeding. Franz held the butcher down on the chopping block and rubbed salt he had grabbed from the salt pork in the meat case into the man's cuts. Mr. O'Kelly's screams brought Mrs. Johnson out of the storeroom. "What's going on here?"

"Mr. O'Kelly fell while he was trying to pay me some money he owes," Franz said.

"Is this another gambling debt?" asked Mrs. Johnson.

"Yes," replied Franz, "a hundred-and-sixty-dollar gambling debt."

"No! It's only a hundred and twenty. I'll pay it someday," said Mr. O'Kelly.

"No," said Franz, "it's a hundred and sixty. There's a forty-dollar collection fee, and I want Daddy Rabbit's money now."

"Daddy Rabbit? You owe Daddy Rabbit? I thought that old man died last year, and you said you quit gambling," said Mrs. Johnson.

"This is a new and younger Daddy Rabbit. He'll be around a long time. I'm Franz Charles. I'm Daddy's collector. I need to be paid today."

"I'm Mrs. Johnson, Mr. O'Kelly's sister," she said as she stuck out her hand for Franz to shake. "I'll have to go across the street to my home to get you the money."

"That will be fine, Mrs. Johnson. May I help you across the street?" Franz asked.

"No, I'll be right back. Have a cold soft drink while you wait. It's on the house."

Franz reached into the cooler for the soft drink and said to Mr. O'Kelly, "Now Mr. O'Kelly, don't be a stranger. Daddy said for you come back anytime and he'll by you a drink."

Franz collected from four people that day. He collected four hundred dollar for Daddy Rabbit and eighty for himself. He did not really have to hurt anyone seriously—a scrape or two, a broken bone or two—nothing really bad. He felt that he would like this new freedom he had at his job, and he was sure he could make some money at it.

Franz met a lot of people. He liked talking to the upper class; they all believed he was royalty from Europe because of his manners and class. He had a touch of a German accent; he spoke the high German of the Swiss. He liked meeting Ashville's upper-class women, educated women, and especially well-dressed women. He enjoyed cooking German food to take on picnics with women. Franz did not like drunk women or loose, trashy women. He liked history and all the things he had studied when he had been with Miss Alice Mauney. He wanted to talk to his dates about some of the history he had studied.

Franz and Daddy Rabbit made a good team. Daddy was smart with the books, and Franz knew how to collect, break bones, and take people's possessions but leave them nonetheless liking him and coming back to Daddy Rabbit's to gamble.

Franz made friends with Dave Morris, who owned La Parisienne, a French restaurant at the Langren Hotel in downtown Asheville. Dave Morris was a gambler. His family was rich and lived in Biltmore Forest. Dave was a pretty nice guy, and Franz liked hanging around with him.

Dave's problem was that he liked to gamble and thought he was good at it, but like most people, he could not beat the house. Dave had a brother-in-law, Ray Davis, who was also a gambler and a drunk. He was a braggart who could not pay his gambling debts; Dave and his father always had to buy him out of trouble. Franz did not like him, but he was a good source of money.

Ray got heavily in debt to Daddy Rabbit. He told Daddy that he was not going to pay him and that there was nothing he could do about it. He said that he and his father-in-law had very heavy political connections who would protect him from Daddy Rabbit if he tried anything. Ray, a real loudmouth, told everybody he had beaten Daddy out of his money.

Daddy told Franz, "You take care of him your special way."

Franz invited Buddy Bryant, an Asheville city policeman, and Dave Morris on a squirrel hunting trip in front of Ray Davis. Ray took the bait and asked if he could come along.

"Sure," said Franz. "Do you know how to hunt?"

That set off one of Ray's tall tales about what a great white hunter he was.

The four men walked all over the mountain and did not shoot a thing. As they crossed the Beaumont Street Bridge, Franz reached under Ray and forced him to the edge of the bridge. He pushed Ray off the bridge onto the pavement below. Ray broke his neck, but he was still breathing when the group got to him. Franz ordered Dave Morris and Buddy Bryant to run down the road to a phone and call for help. As soon as the two men turned to run for help, Franz put him palm over Ray's mouth and pinched his nose closed. Franz looked at him and winked. "I'm going to sleep with your wife." Franz had never met Ray's wife, Dave's sister. He just said that to touché Ray as he died.

At the funeral, Franz met Ray's widow, Suzie Davis. She was five seven, had long, dark hair, and was slim and graceful. She spoke softly and had a large vocabulary. She was an educated, classy woman. She was really sad about her husband, but none of the rest of the family seemed too broken up about it. Franz made out as if he and Ray had been the best of buddies. Ray's family and his wife's family believed it.

That evening, Franz cooked a German dinner for the family. He served Jaeger Schnitzel, Spätzle, gravy with mushrooms, warm red cabbage salad, and an apple pie. Everyone was surprised that a friend of Ray's could cook. Most of his friends the Morris family had met were braggarts, ne'er-do-wells, dandies, men who still lived off their families.

Over the next few months, Dave Morris gave his sister a job at the restaurant as the hostess, bookkeeper, and cleanup girl to get her out of the house and keep her mind active. She and Ray had been married for three years and had lived in a basement apartment at her in-laws. They were nice people and treated her well.

Franz would speak to her when he would go to the restaurant. Dave let Franz into the kitchen to fix special meals when the restaurant closed for the night. Daddy Rabbit would bring in a date, and sometimes, Franz would bring in a date, and the couples would invite Dave and Suzie to join them for Franz's latest culinary creation.

Dave would always say," Let's open a German restaurant. You could run it."

Franz would answer, "I have a job. I love to cook, but I don't think I'd like it for a living. I have to be out and about pattin' and turnin'."

Susie ask Franz what he meant by pattin' and turnin'.

Franz laughed. "Pattin' my foot on a corner and turnin' and walking away."

They all laughed. They were friends who enjoyed each other's company and humor.

One morning, Daddy got a call from a man wanting to know if Daddy wanted to buy some slot machines. "At the right price, sure," replied Daddy. He and the caller worked out a price on the phone.

Daddy, Franz, and the men headed to the Glen Rock Hotel by the train depot. Franz drove around back. They saw no one. Franz started to drive away when a man stepped out from behind a couple of fifty-five-gallon drums. He pointed to two large boxes covered with canvas.

"Those must be the machines," said Daddy. "Pull over to them."

Daddy told Franz, "Stay here till I pay this man. As soon as I do, we'll load up the machines." Franz told the man, "Yes sir! I'll be right there."

Franz drove up close to the machines. Daddy walked over to the man and realized he was wearing a fake nose and mustache and glasses. He turned to Franz. Someone else had stuck a gun in the window of the car at Franz's head.

"Get out of the car," said the man. He was wearing a mask.

As soon as Franz got out of the car, the man hit him in the head with the butt of his gun. Franz went down. He saw that Daddy was taking a whipping. Franz was hit again. The man took his money roll, a couple hundred dollars. They got Daddy's money and the money for the slot machines, a total of about four hundred.

Franz realized he had smelled the man before. He smelled of Bay Rum aftershave and had on brown shoes and black pants.

Franz and Daddy were not in the best of condition to try to get home, so they drove up River Road to Birdeye Plemmons's place, a great café truck stop and gambling house. Birdeye was head of most of the white gambling in the city of Asheville. He was patching up the guys when Franz said he needed a phone. He called his nephew, Leslie, who was in on leave from the navy.

Leslie was the same size as Franz with the same coloring and same good looks. He could have been Franz's twin except for the age difference. Leslie was also Franz's favorite of all his nephews and nieces. Leslie and Franz had hit it off the first they had met. Leslie seemed to talk to Franz about stuff that young men would talk about only to their closest friend. Franz told Leslie, who he called Les, to pick up some first aid stuff and come down to Birdeye's place. Leslie showed up and helped bandage the men.

Franz told Les the story of the fight and the robbery. Leslie drove Daddy home and took Franz home. He snuck Franz into the basement where Franz's room was and helped put him in bed.

Franz got up that evening and got ready to go with Leslie and his new lady friend to dinner. Franz had invited himself to go with them. He told Les he was inviting a friend. Franz said he would pick up the tab. Franz dressed in his best and decided to help Les with his wardrobe. Franz was amazed at how good Leslie looked in his clothes and how well they fit. Franz and Les picked up Les's date, a schoolteacher by the name of Miss Scrounce.

Franz heard her say to Leslie, "You look very sharp tonight. I didn't dress well enough, did I?"

Leslie said, "You look fine." They drove to the Langren Hotel and went into La Parisienne. The hostess sat them and handed them menus. Franz introduced the hostess as Mrs. Suzie Davis, who was his date for the evening. The two couples ate great French food and even better French desserts. They could not pronounce the names, but they were great.

The couples conversed freely. Miss Scrounce told everyone to call her Katie, and Mrs. Suzie Davis told them to call her Suzie. Franz signed the bill. Leslie and Katie went out holding hands.

Suzie Davis said, "Isn't that sweet? They make a great couple."

"So do we," said Franz. "So do we."

Suzie playfully pinched Franz on the arm. "I'll see you later, won't I?"

"Absolutely," replied Franz.

When they got in the car, Franz told Les to take him to the club first and then he could take Katie home and swing back by the club to pick him up.

At the club, Franz told Daddy all about the evening and how nice Miss Katie Scrounce was. Then they planned their move to find out who had robbed them. Franz told Daddy he had a good idea who it was.

"I could smell the man who hit me, and I saw his shoes. I know only one man who puts on Bay Rum and wears brown shoes with black slacks. That fool Joyner, which makes his partner in crime Blalock, that nasty-looking SOB."

"Let me make a few calls and see what's in the air," Daddy said.

Franz called Suzie Davis to tell her what a great time he had had and that Leslie and his lady friend had had a great time also. Franz had never felt about anyone as he felt about Suzie. The thought of her made him warm inside.

Eleven o'clock came, and Dave Morris came into the club. He was one of the eleven o'clock regulars. Franz waved him over and told him the food had been especially good that night and that they had had a good time.

Dave said, "My head chef, John Greene, was on his best game tonight. All my customers told me how good the food was tonight."

Earlier, Daddy had told Franz, "Let me see if I can pinpoint those guys for us tonight." Daddy came back and said, "Got them. Let's go."

Leslie walked into the office with a big grin on his face. Franz waved him over and told him that they had a job to do, that Daddy had found out where the men Franz thought had robbed them were, that they were throwing money around at some of the clubs in West Asheville. Leslie shook Daddy's hand. Daddy said, "Heard you were getting some education tonight, young man."

Leslie looked confused.

Franz slapped Leslie on the back of the head. "He knows you were out with a schoolteacher. My boy, sometimes I think you might be slow." Franz laughed.

"Oh," said Leslie and laughed.

Franz said, "Let's go. We got a job to take care of. Leslie, you're driving. Head to West Asheville. Get onto Haywood Road. Do you know where Creed's bar is?"

"Sure," replied Leslie. "Daddy, you got your new toy with you?"

Daddy Rabbit laughed. "I sure do."

Franz laughed.

The group pulled up outside the bar. Franz said, "Leslie, you drive around back and wait for me. I'll be coming out hot and fast."

Les shrugged his shoulders and nodded.

Franz got out of the car, and as he went into the bar, he hollered, "Where's that stupid damn Joyner and Blalock?" Franz saw the two men run out the backdoor. He ran after them. A large man stood in front of Franz, blocking his way. Franz dropped his shoulder, stuck it into the man's chest, and pushed him over. He stepped over the man and ran out the backdoor. He heard the .45-caliber Thompson submachine gun going off nonstop. He stepped out the door and saw Daddy with the Thompson pointing straight up in the air firing. He saw Leslie jump behind Daddy and grab the gun, but Daddy's gun hand kept firing.

Franz saw one man run down the alley and turn a corner. Franz went after him with the .45 Doyle had left him drawn. Franz saw the man try to turn another corner. He took a knee and squeezed off two shots. One got him in his thigh. The other was a head shot. Joyner hit the ground hard. It did not hurt him because he was dead.

Franz briskly walked to his car. He could see Blalock was dead. He had two or three holes in him, and so did Joyner's car. He saw Daddy and Leslie looking at his car. It had a couple of holes in it as well. "Did that asshole shoot a hole in my car?" Franz asked.

"Uh, no," mumbled Daddy. "I must have hit it when that gun attacked me. Your nephew saved me from that damn Thompson. Thanks, Leslie. Thanks a lot."

Franz was not sure what they were talking about, but knew it was time to leave. He'd find out later.

They asked Leslie to take them back to the club.

Leslie asked Franz, "If I take you back to the club, how will you get home?"

"Les, remember? I have a beautiful Indian Chief at Daddy's. I'll ride it home in the morning."

Franz and Daddy got out at the club. Daddy took his Thompson out of the car. "I'll take this thing to my apartment and put it up before I hurt one of us with it. I didn't know this thing had a mind of its own."

Franz laughed. "I'll meet you in the club."

By the time Daddy got down to the club, Franz was already telling of how Daddy had shot up his car. He left out the part about the two dead gentlemen. Daddy was laughing and saying it could have happened to anyone.

The club was jumping. Everybody was dancing and having a great time. Franz asked Daddy if he would like to play some cards, maybe some tonk, a card game similar to rummy that was played in jazz clubs, military clubs, and colored clubs.

Daddy said, "No, I'm too wired up after all the excitement tonight. Aren't you wired? How can you play after tonight?"

"Wired? No. To me it's just part of the job. You sure you don't want to play?" asked Franz.

"No, I'm good." Daddy admired Franz for always remaining calm.

Franz thought more about the large man he had dropped with that shoulder butt. *Damn. That big boy went down like a sack of wet cement. Man, I'm in good shape. I wonder if I could take up boxing again.*

Boxing was an athletic endeavor Franz had tried after he had gotten out of the military brig and the army. He had found out quickly he did not like boxing. He did not like not breaking bones or cutting his opponents. He did not like three-minute rounds. He did not like other men hitting him. He did not like letting a man up off the floor after he had knocked him down. He had had to fight the urge to stomp his opponents on the ground. He liked to watch boxing and bet on it, but he had no desire any longer to participate directly in the sport.

He wanted to put on wrestling matches between naked women. He bet he could sell tickets for that. He wondered what it would look like for Miss Katie Scrounce, Leslie's teacher friend, to wrestle Mrs. Suzie Davis naked. He was going cross-eyed thinking about it. He had to stop or faint. *Damn. That would be something.*

Daddy asked Franz, "Why are you sweating so much? Here's your list to collect tonight. You sure you're okay? You look flushed."

"No, man, I'm okay. Just thinking to myself." He would have been embarrassed if anyone had read his thoughts.

Franz had to collect at the Glen Rock Hotel that night. Many traveling salesmen stayed there because it was across the street from the train depot. Trains were salesmen's main form of transportation. They liked to gamble, drink, and chase women. They generally ended up at Daddy Rabbit's place. They had a good time as they lost all their money. Franz had to check on them at the Glen Rock to keep them from sneaking out of town owing Daddy money.

Franz got Daddy about two hundred, and he got himself forty-five. He had only one hard case he had to remind of his debt. He had had to chase this overweight man of fifty or so up and down two floors of the hotel. He caught up with him in the kitchen. The kitchen help knew who Franz was, so they stayed out of his way. Some of them would see him later that night at Daddy's. The man was out of breath and looked as if were about to have a heart attack.

Franz grabbed him. "You look like hell. Sit here and have some water. Let's talk about it. Hey! Get this guy some water. Also, when I leave, I need a couple of roast beef sandwiches and some French fries. Let me have some of those bananas too," yelled Franz, who turned back to the overweight man. "Now sir, where is the money?"

"I don't have it right now."

"How much do you have right now?"

"Just twenty. That's to get home on."

"Okay. Here's what we're going to do. You give me ten dollars now. In two weeks, when you come back to Asheville, you'll need to pay Daddy the fifty you owe him and a thirty-dollar fine for being late. If you run, I'll come to your hometown and burn you house down and bury you under the rubble. I can find you through your company. You know that, right?"

"Yes sir."

Franz gave the man a glass of water and helped him up. "You do know you're still welcome to come to Daddy Rabbit's and drink and gamble."

"Thank you sir." Franz and Daddy knew that this guy, just like many others, was going to gamble somewhere. They wanted him to gamble and drink with them. If one of these guys actually won any one night, Daddy would toast him and tell everybody in the club how good of a gambler he was and how lucky he was, that this could happen to anyone.

Daddy and Franz knew that as long as that man and others stayed loyal to their club, they would eventually lose. They all did.

Franz was such a gentleman when he had to collect even when he had to get rough. The gamblers still liked him, and they seemed not to take it personally. Franz would always talk to each one and make him feel as if he were the most important person in the world. He always complimented their lady friends they brought to the club. If Franz saw the men outside the club, he always shook their hands and graciously greeted them. Franz talked so well and dressed and looked so good that people liked being around him. He would never embarrass anyone in front of others even if they owed Daddy money.

Franz always danced with the families of the gamblers. He was a great dancer. In Miami a few years back, a dance studio owed money to Daddy, so Franz took dance lessons for some of the debt. Franz took jujitsu lesson for three years to collect the full fee for the master's debt. The master said he was good enough to fight professionally.

Franz liked making himself the best he could be. He liked that he had a bit of a Swiss or German accent. He had been only two when he came to America, but his dad had made sure he and his siblings spoke German. He had his nails buffed and cleaned by a professional. He had his hair cut weekly. He looked and acted like a sissy model, but he always surprised people with just how rough and mean he could be if absolutely necessary.

Once, Franz had to collect a very large debt from an upper-crust attorney who had decided not to pay. Franz had to go to the man's golf club one evening during a dance to find the man. Franz went to his table. The attorney had seven others at the table, four couples. Franz asked to see the attorney in private. The attorney said, "Get lost, you pansy, before I beat the hell out of you." The others at the table laughed. Franz laughed too. He winked at the people and grabbed the man's hand and stuck it in steak sauce and bit off half of the man's little finger. He spit it in the wife's drink.

"I'll come by your house tomorrow to collect the money and the fee. The fee will now be a hundred dollars plus the rest of the money. Would one of you people help this man to the hospital? Can't you see he's in pain?" Franz wiped his mouth on the wife's napkin and left. The next day, the attorney paid Franz all the money and apologized to Franz for all the trouble. Franz asked the man how his family was doing and shook the man's hand as if they were good friends.

Every big-time gambling house in the city and county offered Franz jobs, and some offered him a piece of the action if he would leave Daddy Rabbit's and come with them. Nobody knew how close Daddy Rabbit and Franz were or how long they had been together and the trust they had in each other, stronger than family.

Franz could not even spend the money he had. He started giving Brigitta an extra dollar a week for his room. He also paid Ruth and her sister, Laura Ann, a dollar a week apiece. He wanted clean sheets on his bed every day, and he liked his shirts lightly starched. He showed them how to iron his shirts the way he liked, and they started ironing all the family shirts Franz's way. Even Daddy Rabbit began to send his shirts with Franz to have Ruth and her sister do for him just as they did for Franz. Daddy would send them a dollar fifty apiece weekly.

Every so often, when a grocery store owner would lose too much money, Franz would have to take a whole beef filet or a shoulder or a standing rib roast home as some of his fee. Franz would take Suzie to Otto and Brigitta's home for special occasions.

He always looked and acted the perfect gentleman around Suzie, who liked Franz a lot. She did not know of his dark side. Dave Morris and Suzie would take him to their family functions. Suzie's parents would always comment, "Franz is a perfect gentleman. It's about time Suzie finally met a man of culture. He's probably a European aristocrat. You can always tell a man of class and good breeding."

Suzie's parents also liked the fact that Dave had quit hanging out with gamblers and prostitutes. They had not had to bail him out of jail since he had started hanging out with the upper-crust Franz Charles. They were glad Suzie's first husband had died in a hunting accident before he got her pregnant. They were sure he had been trying to show off in front of Franz when he fell.

They thought that where Franz had come from, gentlemen knew how to act on a hunt. They knew how to dress for a hunt. They thanked God that stupid Ray Davis hadn't hurt Franz or their son, Dave, with his antics. Mrs. Morris felt she could hold her head up again at the woman's club since that stupid Ray Davis was out of their family.

Many women who had met Franz Charles thought he was an outstanding young man. He had the air of having graduated from an ivy league college up north. Others were convinced he had been educated in Europe. No one suspected he had not graduated from high school.

Franz also enjoyed teaching his nephews how to wrestle and box. He also taught them how to street fight. Franz, Leslie, and Daddy Rabbit went out and practiced with the Thompson and the Colt .45. All three became very good with the weapons, Franz especially with the Thompson.

About that time, Franz began to feel the clock ticking as far as marriage and children were concerned. He did not look it or feel it—he was just in the midthirties—but he knew he was getting older and felt lonely.

Otto and Brigitta began to expect Suzie Davis at all their family functions. The kids already thought of her as family. Otto had his big brother talk to Franz about family and settling down. Otto knew what Franz did for a living. He knew Franz's reputation. Otto told Franz he could get him on at the railroad, he could get him on as the head chef on a diner car to Miami and back. Or Franz could open a German restaurant in any of the finer hotels in and around Asheville; Otto and Brigitta would put up some of the money.

Franz said he would think about it. He considered it a good idea, but he wondered what he would do about Daddy Rabbit. They worked well together, they trusted each other, and they depended on each other. Franz could not just quit on Daddy. And Franz did not know if he really wanted to cook every day or run a restaurant. Maybe with Suzie's help they could be successful. He would think about it, let the idea work around his brain for a while. He would keep his eye open for a place for a good, upscale European restaurant. He had some time.

CHAPTER 10

Suzie Davis

"Franz? Franz?" *Knock, knock.* "Franz! It's Daddy. Wake up, Franz." *Knock, knock.* Franz was up and jerking open the door to his bedroom.

"What the hell's going on?" Franz screamed.

He saw Otto, Brigitta, and Daddy Rabbit in the hallway in the basement. "What's going on?" he asked again.

Otto put his arm around Franz. "Mr. Rabbit has some bad news for you."

If it's bad news from Daddy Rabbit, it's not anything to do with the family. But what could it be? "What is it, Daddy?" asked Franz.

"I have some bad news about Miss Suzie," said Daddy.

Franz grabbed Daddy's arm. "What? What's the matter with her? Is she okay?"

"This is from the police, so I'm not sure how accurate it is," Daddy said, "but it seems there were some construction men from the North Carolina Highway Department drinking in their room at the Langren. When they decided to find a place to eat, they went down to La Parisienne. Miss Suzie was locking the front door when the men walked up and demanded she open up for them. She told them she couldn't do that, so they pushed her inside and went in behind her and locked the door. Miss Suzie ran through the restaurant. They cornered her in the kitchen. They beat her up pretty bad, and then the three men raped her. She's in bad shape at Memorial Mission Hospital on Woodfin. We'll take you there now."

"Oh no!" Franz cried. He dressed frantically. The four drove to the hospital. Suzie's parents were there. The doctor told them that only her parents could see her then, that she was going to be physically okay. He said she had a broken arm and a lot of bruises and cuts and scrapes, but that would all heal in time.

Dave, Franz, Brigitta, Otto, and Daddy Rabbit were in the waiting room for the rest of the day. At about four that afternoon, the doctor told them they could see her for a minute but to not get her excited. Each of them went in to say hello and say they were thinking about her. Franz went in last. While Franz was in Suzie's room, a nurse asked the Morrises who the colored man was.

Mrs. Morris looked at Daddy. "I'm not sure who he is. I think maybe he's the Charleses' chauffeur."

A policeman came in then and said, "No, that's Daddy Rabbit, a nightclub owner and big-time gambler and bookie. What's he doing here?"

The Morrises said they did not know. They thought maybe he was the one who had found Suzie. They were sure he had nothing to do with the Morrises.

"Hey Daddy Rabbit, why are you here? Do you know these people?" the policeman asked.

"Yes, Officer. Miss Suzie is the lady friend of my partner, Mr. Franz Charles."

The Morrises looked at each other and knew what the other was thinking: *How is it that Mr. Franz Charles, a European aristocrat, is mixed up with a colored gambler? Maybe he finances this colored man. Yes, that has to be it.*

When Franz came out of the room, the policeman said, "Damn. Someone's in trouble. That one's crazy. He's the muscle for that colored gangster."

Franz asked the Officer if the police had any clues as to who had done this. The Officer said, "We've questioned three men, but we couldn't hold them. They said they didn't do it, and we had to believe them. The father of one works for the governor, and the other is the nephew of the head of the state police. We're sure they did it, but there's no way to prove it. Now if you'll excuse me, I need to talk to the young lady."

Franz felt violated himself. He was so angry and confused about what to do. He had never felt that bad before and did not know how to act or express his feelings. He could feel white heat coming over his body. He thought he would faint. He could not catch his breath. He thought of Suzie lying in that hospital bed all bandaged up, bruises on her face. Her voice had been like that of a scared child. She had apologized to Franz, for what he did not know. She had been the victim. A scared and hurt victim.

Franz stayed at the hospital as long as he could. The hospital made him go home at eight o'clock. He and Daddy went to the club. Franz asked Daddy to find out who and where these guys were. Daddy had connections at the police department.

The Morrises took their daughter home the next day. The doctors had felt she would feel better at home with her mother's cooking. That afternoon, Franz went over to the Morrises and sat with Suzie. Brigitta brought a basket of food Ruth had made.

Franz told Suzie to listen to him without interruption. Suzie agreed. "Suzie, you're the first person I've ever loved. You make me feel like a whole person. Our days together at the Langren in our special room were the best times I've ever spent in my life. When we made love, I knew we were in love. When we made love, I knew I wanted no other woman in my life. I love sitting in the room by the window and reading with you. We both love to read about the great love affairs in history.

"I've often wondered why I'm the way I am. I think it's from not having a birth mother. Now don't get me wrong. Stella was the nicest person to me. I know she loved me and tried to raise me the best she could. Other kids where we lived picked on me every day. My father worked all the time, and the only one to take care of me was Otto.

"Otto had to go to work too, and I was left alone with John and Etta. I loved them, and they loved me, but they didn't know any more than I did. I stayed out in the woods most of the time by myself. I got hungry and ate bugs and worms. The neighborhood kids would see me doing this and call me names and beat me up. Sometimes, they would pee on me.

"I got bigger and stronger, and I was finally able to take care of myself. I learned to fight and win. I learned to never show fear. I was never as smart as my brothers and sister. They could all play musical instruments, not me, and that disappointed my dada.

"My grades in school were never as good as my siblings' grades. Dad had taught them to speak, read, and write German, but all I could do was speak and understand it. I was never able to read or write it. I always felt I was a second-class person, a real loser. It took a long time for me to learn to respect myself.

"I learned to respect myself after meeting Daddy Rabbit, who has always treated me as an equal, and seeing how my family has been successful and hard-working, and finally meeting you, a beautiful and educated woman who cares for and loves me and whom I really care for and love. I'm not sure if this is the right time to tell you, but I don't know when the right time would be, so I need to tell you now if we're to have a life together."

"What do you need to tell me?" asked Suzie in a scared girl's voice.

"Suzie, I was with your husband when he passed away."

"I know."

"Suzie, I pushed him off the bridge. It wasn't an accident. Please don't hate me."

Suzie jerked her hand from his and stared at him. Tears started down her cheeks.

Franz stood. "I'll let you get some rest." He left.

Franz went to the club. Daddy saw him and waved him over. "How's Miss Suzie, today?"

"She's going to be fine."

"I got the information you asked for."

"Tell me everything you found out," said Franz.

Daddy told a girl who worked for him to bring a couple of steaks and potatoes and beer to his private table. He and Franz sat.

"There's three of them. They work for the highway department. They're up here looking at highway rights of way. They're well connected politically. Most of the time when they're not working, they stay up in their rooms and drink and play cards. All three went to state college. Two are married with kids. The father-in-law of one owns a bunch of textile mills in the eastern part of the state. He's well connected. Whatever you're going to do, I'll be right with you."

"I know, Daddy. Let me get out of here for a while. I'll let you know. I have to do some thinking. I'll be at Suzie's parents' home in Biltmore Forest. Could you pick me up about seven this morning?"

"I'll be there," Daddy Rabbit said.

Daddy drove up to the Davis home right on time and blew the horn. Franz walked out of the bushes and got into Daddy's car. As they drove off, Daddy asked, "Are you okay? What happened last night? You left and didn't come back."

"I went to Otto's for my money. I'd hid it in the basement there. I have it. I want to give it to you to give to Suzie and Otto. Give Suzie sixteen thousand and the rest, four thousand, to Otto. Will you do that for me?"

"Yes, but why don't you give it to them yourself?"

"I can't go around them anymore."

"Why's that?"

"I went to the hotel early this morning and knocked on the door of one of the men who jumped Suzie. I told him I was with the hotel and had to check the steam pipes. He was drunk and half asleep. He was in a double room. His partner was in bed passed out. As he walked back into the room, I kicked him behind the knee, and he went down. I grabbed his hair and pulled his head back and told him who I was. I took my hawk-billed knife and cut his throat. As he lay gurgling on the floor, I woke up his roommate and told him who I was and what I had just done. I cut his throat. I went down the hall and knocked on the other man's door. I told him I had some bad news for him about his friends. I told him I was hotel security and told him to follow me to the other room. When we went in, he saw his friends and threw up. Damn, what a mess. I told him that the gentleman friend of the lady he and his partners had beaten and raped had just done this to his friends.

"He asked me what I was going to do about it. I told him I was going to do the same to him. He tried to run, but I caught him and cut his throat. As I left the hotel, a bellboy and the night clerk saw me. I went straight to Suzie's house and sat on her bed until she woke. I told her that nobody was going to hurt her now and that I loved her. I told her that I wouldn't see her for a while and that you would tell her how I was doing. I gave her my car and tried to hug her, but she just looked at me and didn't say a thing. Here we are."

"What are you going to do now? And how?"

"I don't know where I'm going, but I have to go before the police come after me. I'm going to ride my Indian Chief. She's fast and can go where a car cannot."

Daddy Rabbit helped Franz put on his leather gloves and leather jacket. He helped tie Franz's luggage on his motorcycle and gave Franz a big hug. "You take it easy, my brother. I'll watch everything here for you. Damn. I'm going to miss you. Stay safe and keep it on the road." Daddy Rabbit felt tears coming down his cheeks. As far as he knew, it was the first time he had ever cried.

Franz hugged him and said good-bye. He put on his cap and sped away toward Mars Hill to see his folks and family. He told his dad what had happened. He told him the whole story, the truth. It was perhaps the first time in his life that he had told his dad the truth. It made him feel clean inside. He hugged his family. He thought it might have been the last time he would ever do that. He got on his Indian, rode to the Mississippi, and turned north.

CHAPTER 11

The Trip North

Franz rode all night not knowing where he was going. For the first time in his life, he felt lost, alone. He wondered about the rest of his life, which was new for him. He had never thought about a future, about what he would do with his life; he had just done stuff.

He thought about Suzie. He cried when he thought about what those men had done to her, how they had hurt her. He would get angry and sad at the thought he might not see her again. He wanted to kill those men's families. He felt bad about not being able to say good-bye to Otto. Franz thought there was no finer man than Otto.

It started to rain. Franz found shelter under a railroad trestle in East Saint Louis, Illinois. He saw that the bus station in East Saint Louis was busy day and night. He decided to get a room and a job to keep his mind busy because this thinking about what could have been was driving him crazy.

Franz rode to the bus station and parked his Indian. He started walking in large squares around East Saint Louis looking for a rooming house that would let him park his motorcycle in a garage. Franz hit every bar, pool hall, and gambling joint he could find. He just could not get excited about working in anyone of them. East Saint Louis was wide open to all the vices at that time, but Franz was not interested. *I don't want to be a gangster anymore. It's time I did something good with my life, but what? I'm not trained to do anything but break bones. That woman has ruined my life. She has me thinking I could be somebody. She has me thinking about a future. Damn, I miss her. Is my future with her?*

My nephew wrote me about our cousins in Hawaii owning a gift shop and living by the beach. Suzie and I could do that, but how? I want to see her, but how? Am I capable of living the good life with a good woman and having an honest job? I've never had one. We're in a depression, and there are no jobs except for what I do best, being a gangster. Suzie and I don't want that kind of life. I didn't tell her of my transformation to an honest man. Am I going to be one? I have to shut my brain off before I go crazy.

Franz wanted to call home but knew he could not. He knew the police were looking for him. He had not tried to hide the fact he had killed those men. He needed to stay hidden for a long time. He wandered East Saint Louis for days trying to figure things out. He wandered into the lunch counter at the bus station for breakfast when he saw a notice advertising for a night manager. *I could do that.* He asked the counter girl if he could speak to the manager about the job. She screamed to the backroom for the manager. A man in a white apron and white paper soda jerk hat came out. "You the one looking for the job?"

"Yes. I saw your sign."

"We need someone to run the night shift. Starts at eleven and ends at seven. Ten dollars a week and all you can eat. There are four buses that come in at night, and sometimes, the passengers are hungry. We have a regular crowd of taxi drivers who hang out here and a couple of cops who come in two, three times a night. It'll be clean when you get here and clean when you leave. You work six nights then off one. You work alone. You come in clean and sober. Try not to drink on the job. You can't feed your friends or relatives for free. Nobody using our tables for gambling. You want the job?"

Boy, have I come down in this world. Do people really live like this? Do I really want a job this badly? But if I work here, nobody will care who I am. It will give me time to clear my head.

"Yes, I'll take the job."

"Okay. You start tonight. Come in at ten thirty. I'll show you what to do. Do you have a police record?"

"No. Never been in trouble."

Franz then had to find a place to stay. He found a rooming house on a quiet street. He reported to work that evening dressed and ready to work. His new boss showed him how to run the cash register and to cook what was on the menu, basic food—eggs, bacon, sausage, pancakes, hash browns, soup, gravy, BLTs, hamburgers, fries, toast, hotdogs. They also served cake, pies, and ice cream. Franz thought he could handle it as long as nobody crossed him. The hours went by.

The days and weeks went by. Franz had made a few friends among the taxi drivers, bus drivers, city workers, and bus mechanics. He learned to talk sports and politics with the night people. There was always a drunk or two to sober up, a brokenhearted man or woman who had just got dumped to listen to.

Franz liked talking to the military guys as they passed through East Saint Louis going to a new assignment or heading home. Franz liked their stories of the foreign cities and people. The soldiers talked about how they were going to war and how they would win it.

He liked talking to the bus drivers and the stories they told about their passengers. He began to think he liked these stories too much. He was afraid of becoming a daydreamer rather than a doer. He wanted to be the one talked about, not the one listening.

He learned that one of the bus companies had added Asheville to its route. There were more and more people for the south coming north to Saint Louis, right across the Mississippi, for factory jobs. He figured somebody would sooner or later recognize him. He had to start watching more closely at the passengers getting off the buses coming from the south.

He had made only one call to Daddy Rabbit to let him know he was alive and okay. He wanted Daddy to tell Otto and Suzie he was okay and was thinking about them. He wanted to see everyone but could not go home yet.

Franz asked Daddy if the police were looking for him.

"They come in about every day looking for you. They've taken me down to the station three time trying to sweat your whereabouts out of me. They've talked to Otto and his wife a couple of times, and they've talked to Miss Suzie a couple of times. We're sure they check where our mail comes from, so don't write or send cards. You need anything? Except if you did, I don't know how we'd get it to you."

"Thanks, Daddy. I'll keep in touch." Franz went back to being lonely.

The next night at work, Franz saw a gambler he had had to collect money from hard in Asheville a couple of times. The man was a traveling salesman, and it looked like East Saint Louis had become part of his territory. He had to make sure the man did not see him. He kept his head down and tried to talk as little as possible.

The next morning, he told the manager he had a family emergency and had to leave. The manager told Franz he was the best help he had ever had work for him. "Mr. Isaiah Morris, I will surly miss you. I hope everything is okay at home. By the way, where is home?"

"Texas. Texas."

Franz packed and hit the road for Chicago. He knew it would be harder to find anyone in a city the size of Chicago.

On his ride to Chicago, he tried to think of what he should do. He needed a place to hide that was not out in the open, somewhere that was not the crossroads of town. He needed a place where he would blend in. He also needed a place to store his beloved Indian. Suzie had loved it as much as he did.

Franz got into Chicago at midnight and rode the streets until seven. He tried to remember everything his nephew Leslie had told him about Chicago. Leslie had taken his basic training for the navy at the Great Lakes Training Facility north of Chicago, and his first duty assignment had been there. Leslie had said hundreds of civilians worked on base and rode buses back and forth to work. The facility offered basic training and schools for all the jobs in the navy. It also had a large number of permanent navy staff.

Not only was Chicago crowed, but so was North Chicago because of the base. Franz was sure he could get lost there. He found a boarding house with a shed for his Indian. It was close to the bus routes and stores. He then had to get a job. He rode around for a few days trying to decide what would be his next adventure in the job market. He had actually liked being the night manager at the lunch counter.

Franz decided to try for a job on the naval base. He went to the civilian personnel office to see what they had. The only openings available for nonskilled labor were in the mess halls. He had not liked

KP when he was in the army and was sure he would not like it on base, but he needed a job. *I'll try this. I'll look around for another job at the same time. At least it will be something to do and somewhere to go every day.*

He got the job. The navy gave him work boots he had to keep clean and polished. He received white shirts and pants. He would get a clean white apron and paper soda jerk hat daily. The navy wanted the civilian work force clean-shaven, but he could have a mustache. Franz told the mess's master chief petty Officer that he had experience with breakfasts and German foods. He told Franz he would have to work his way up to the day shift. They had openings only on the midnight chow shift.

"What's the midnight chow shift?" asked Franz.

"You come to work at twenty-one hundred hours and work until oh seven hundred hours. You serve what chow was left over from supper, and you serve breakfast all night long. There will be twenty-one men on the midnight shift. There's four enlisted men, a master chief, an Officer, and sixteen of you civilians. Here's your stuff. Be on time, sober, and dressed clean and neat."

"Thank you, Chief."

That evening, Franz started his new career as a civilian cook for the navy. He kept the name Isaiah Morris. Franz liked his new job. He especially liked working around the navy men and the marines. *I hated the military when I was in it, but now, I really enjoy being around it. Strange.*

What Franz had matured to like about the military was the strict discipline and the cleanliness. He liked being around the lifers; Franz gained respect for these men. He realized he was beginning to act and feel as if he were in the military. And he was beginning to like himself again, this time as a regular man, not a gangster.

The days and weeks sped by, and Franz was becoming more settled into his new life. He went out drinking and partying with some of his new friends; all three were in the navy. They took him to a club on the base for noncommissioned officers. This club always had plenty of women to dance and socialize with. Because of the Depression, most men did not have the money to take women out and show them a good time, so many women came to the military clubs, where the military men had plenty of money and liked to spend it on them.

The base had movie theaters, skating rinks, bowling alleys, dance clubs, pool halls, cafés, and bars—lots of places to have a good time. Franz and his friends would dance and drink for hours. One evening, they decided to shoot some pool. In the pool room, they met four women. Franz ended up with someone named Maude. *Strange. I've heard that name before. I think I heard it around here. But where?* It hit him. *From Leslie! I wonder if this is the same girl—no, it couldn't be. That would be too strange.*

It was twenty-two hundred hours. Franz had to get ready for work. He told his friends good night and headed out. Maude followed him out the pool hall, grabbed him, and kissed him. "I'll be here next Friday night," she said. "Let's meet at nineteen thirty hours here and spend the evening together."

"Okay. It's a date."

He walked to the mess hall, washed his face, changed his clothes, and rinsed his mouth with vinegar to get rid of the beer smell. He had bacon and eggs and started to work. The mess hall was full and stayed that way most of the night. Sailors would come in for chow after their dates or their times at the clubs. It seemed that sailors who had been drinking could always put away some chow.

Franz deboned a couple dozen fried pork chops and made a light-brown gravy. He made potato pancakes from leftover mashed potatoes and onions. He chopped up some chard, beet greens, and braised it in water with salt, pepper, garlic, and oil. He baked some ageing pears with butter and cheese. At about four in the morning, he served his working companions German-style pork chops and gravy over potatoes and onions, braised Swiss chard, and baked pears. The Officer, the enlisted men, and the civilians in the mess hall loved Franz's cooking. He was then allowed to take whatever leftovers he wanted to play with and reconstruct then into gourmet meals.

He surprised his coworkers every day. He would mash leftover boiled potatoes and add butter, crumbled bacon, peas or pintos, onions, a chopped meat of some sort, and cheese and serve it with gravy. The men wanted it every day. One of Franz's new friends was the pastry chef, the Dessert Queen as the others called him, who taught Franz to create great desserts.

The following Friday night, Franz had to decide whether to meet Maude at the NCO club. He just did not feel like meeting a woman just then in his life. That made him feel strange. He had always had a woman. He did not think he could have ever lived without one. *Has Suzie killed my desire for other woman? Will I be alone for the rest of my life?*

Franz got ready to meet his military friends at the club. He decided to let the evening progress as it was supposed to, though he was not sure what that would be. At the club, he saw Maude with her girlfriends waiting for them. "Let's start with some beer and find a table," one of his friends said. The couples sat around the table talking over the week's events. Franz asked Maude some leading questions to find out if she was Leslie's Maude, but she wasn't telling him anything he could use to determine that. When he asked if she had children, she said, "I came here for fun! Let's dance. You can dance, can't you?" She pulled him to the dance floor.

Franz decided to be a little more subtle in his questioning of Maude. He also decided to show the place how well he could dance after all his years of dance lessons. He and Maude danced two songs and came back to the table. The group had decided Franz had been a professional dancer in the past. All the women at the table wanted to dance with him, and he obliged them.

At twenty two hundred hours, Franz said he was going to work. Maude followed him outside again and grabbed Franz and kissed him again. This time, she also grabbed his manhood and asked if he was sure he had to go to work.

This shocked him for a few seconds. "I work every Friday night. I'm off only on Saturday nights."

"I come to the base only on Friday nights. I'm not ever going to have any fun with you, am I? See you around, big boy." She left.

Franz headed to work. *She has to be Leslie's Maude. I can't wait to tell him I met her.*

Franz got to work and found some marines on a work detail for being insubordinate. They were painting the chow hall. The chief told

Franz to make sure he prepared enough of his special food to feed the four marines. Franz saw that the marines were not clean-shaven. Their hair was too long and unkempt, their boots were not spit-shined, and their work uniforms were not starched or ironed very well. He had worked at the base long enough to be able to tell all the ranks and rates of the navy and marines. He could recognize good and bad troops, and he could tell these four were bad marines. Franz wondered if that was the way he had been in the army. *I sure hope not. These men are a disgrace to the corps. Damn. Why should I care how they look? But I do.*

Later that morning—lunchtime for the mess hall staff—Franz served what he called his Mexican pie. It started with a thin layer of corn bread, then a layer of spiced ground beef, a layer of cheese, a layer of pinto beans, another layer of ground beef, a layer of canned tomatoes, and then chopped green chilies. Franz sat with Matt Summers, one of the marines, to eat. He and Matt had a long talk.

Matt was from a factory town outside Detroit. He had gotten into trouble with the police. He had built up a reputation for breaking and entering city offices and going through the employees' desks and lockers for money and food. On his forth arrest, the judge told him he could go into the Marines or work on the prison road gangs. He had chosen the Marines.

He had never been a good marine. He was starting his fourth year of a six-year enlistment. He had just received orders to ship out to China. He had never adjusted to the discipline and rigors of the military. He was always late, tired, or sick. He could never look or act like a marine with the spit and polish that required. Matt had spent four years doing day labor or punishment duties. He had never gone on a tour overseas or even to another country. He had spent his time in the Great Lakes area or the East Coast. He did not want to go to China. He wanted out of the Marines.

Franz felt sorry for him. He remembered having the same attitude when he was in the army. Franz tried to tell the twenty-eight-year-old Matt that he could tough it out for his remaining two years.

The marine paint crew worked in the mess hall for a week and then outside the mess hall for another week. Franz had spent a lot of that time with Matt trying to help him understand that he could not just quit the Marines and go home, that he would end up in the brig. Franz met him after work and showed him how much fun stuff there was to do on base, but Matt was just too depressed to care.

On his last day of painting detail, Matt tried to cut his wrists. Franz had caught him and stopped him. "Why are you doing this?"

"I have to report to San Diego in thirty-one days to ship overseas, but I'm not going," he replied. He started crying.

Franz took Matt to his apartment and bandaged his wrist. He told him to get some shut-eye; he said things would look better in the morning. Franz made himself a sandwich and some tea. He sat outside his little apartment and dozed. He dreamed of being a marine and having a marine wedding with Suzie. He would go back over how he had gotten where he was and how he needed to restart his life. He wondered if Suzie would ever forgive him for killing her husband. He could feel himself smothering the man again and what he had told him as he died: "I'm going sleep with your wife." *I could use a new life and a new start. I could do that in China in the Marines. The police would never look for me there. I bet I could pull this off.*

He woke Matt and told him they were going to change identities. Franz would become Matt and ship out to China. Matt could go home as someone else. Matt told Franz that most of his family was in Canada and that he could disappear up there. Matt cried and thanked Franz over and over.

Franz had Matt tell him everything he had done in the Marines, everybody he knew or had met, any fights he had been in, and all the times he was in trouble, what had caused it, and how he gotten out of it or the punishment he had received for it. He learned everywhere Matt had been. He learned about the places Matt had been stationed.

Franz wanted to know about the military occupation school Matt had attended and what he had trained for. Matt had attended the marine rifle school and a transportation school. Franz read and reread the marine manual and practiced all the marine moves. He had been watching the marines for many months. He knew how to be a marine.

Franz turned in his notice to the chow hall. He told everyone he had to leave to take care of his ageing parents. He went to the barber on base and got a marine flattop haircut. He went to the uniform store and purchased a complete set of marine uniforms with shoes and all the brass. He had all the uniforms tailored and ironed marine style. He booked a seat on the train for Matt that would take him to Canada. He gave Matt all his clothes and a hundred dollars.

They talked about how Matt would blend in and disappear in Canada. Franz told Matt he could never be Matt again and would have to stay in Canada the rest of his life and stay out of trouble.

Franz packed all his marine gear and a few civilian things and strapped it to his Indian. He rode around the base and the Chicago area. He felt he was leaving and old friend. He had felt safe there. He turned the Indian south and headed to Asheville.

Franz daydreamed on his way to Asheville about the past year and all the changes that had occurred in his life. He thought about his new friends. He was actually going to miss them. He thought about how much he had liked his job at the chow hall. He had liked cooking and making up recipes for his versions of Swiss cooking. He wondered if he could pull off being ten years younger and in a marine rifle company. But even if he did not like it, he would be out in a year and a half. He wondered if he could run into Leslie, who was a sailor in China then.

Franz's mind raced as fast as he raced the roads to get home to Asheville. As he got closer to Asheville, he tried to figure out how he would get to see everybody without getting caught. He rode to the train depot and went into the teletype office. There was Otto. "Hey, big brother," he shouted. Otto had to stare a second or two before he believed it was Franz.

Otto rushed over and hugged Franz. "What are you doing here? You okay? Did anyone see you?" He laughed and hugged Franz again.

"I'll tell you all about it, but let me get you to make a call for me, okay?"

"Sure. Who do you want me to call?"

Franz gave Otto Daddy Rabbit's number. "Tell him you have a package for him at the depot, that it's from Doyle. He'll know what that means. Then I want you to call Dave Morris at the restaurant and tell him Daddy said he was going to pick up his sister."

"Sure," said Otto. "Can I call Brigitta too?"

"Please do. You have a place for me to freshen up?"

"Sure. We have a shower and everything here."

Otto made the calls while Franz showered and put on his dress uniform, hat and all.

Daddy Rabbit and Suzie arrived at the same time Brigitta did. When they entered Otto's office, Franz stepped out of the changing room in full uniform. No one recognized him at first. Suzie saw who he was and ran to him. Otto said, "Damn! You look good. But it's against the law to dress like a marine if you're not one."

CHAPTER 12

Marine? I Am One

"**M**arine? I am one," Franz replied.

Daddy Rabbit hugged Franz. "It's good to see you, brother. You look good. Boy, I wish the club could see you now."

Brigitta hugged Franz and had to wipe her eyes. Suzie kept hugging him.

"Everybody sit. I'll tell you my story," Franz said.

He spent a couple of hours telling his story, and Franz was a good storyteller. Everyone was amazed. He told them of his assignment to China, how it would be only a year and a half, and that he would look up Leslie. He said he thought he might be able to come back to Asheville as Matt Summers with a clean record.

"Otto, I want you to take my Indian home with you. It's yours or give it to one of the boys, okay? Daddy, will you pick me up a couple of steaks with all the trimming from John Greene at La Parisienne? Brigitta, will you pick up Suzie here in the morning and take her home? Otto, do you mind if Suzie and I stay in your office tonight to talk about our future?"

"Franz, this office stays open all night. The night crew uses it. I'll get you a room at the Glen Rock Hotel across the street in the name of the president of the railroad and his guest. I've reserved a seat on the train going west at seven in the morning for you if that's okay."

"Thanks, Otto," Franz said gratefully.

That evening, Franz and Suzie made honeymooners' love with each other. They made French love with each other. They also talked most of the night away about their future together. They ate their steaks and drank champagne while talking about their families and how they may want one themselves. They did not talk about Suzie's dead husband or Suzie's attackers Franz had killed.

That morning, Franz put on his class-A uniform. Suzie told him she liked it best. He packed and said good-bye to Suzie in the hotel. They were afraid of being seen together outside or someone recognizing Franz. Franz hugged and kissed her as she cried. Franz wanted to cry also. He hugged and said good-bye to Otto. He told him he would keep in touch.

Suzie called Franz her husband.

Franz boarded the train and sat beside a marine Captain and across from two second lieutenants. *Now's the time to see if I can pull this off.* The Captain asked Franz his name and where he was going. "Private Matt Summers, sir. I'm headed to China sir, Shanghai."

"What's your rating, Private?" asked the Captain.

"Just a grunt rifleman sir."

"We're going there also, Private," said the Captain.

Franz decided to try out his new life story to see if it was believable. "Captain, how long have you been in the Marines? And where have you been stationed, sir?"

The Captain had been in for ten years. He had been assigned to Nicaragua, Panama, China, Cherry Point in North Carolina, and Camp Lejeune in North Carolina. The Captain asked Private Matt Summers where he had been stationed. Franz remembered the places Matt had told him about.

"Sir, I was assigned to Cherry Point, Camp Lejeune, and the Great Lakes Training Facility. Sir, it took me a long time to grow up and appreciate the Marine Corps. I was never a good marine. I think I was depressed most of the time. You see, sir, I was put into the Marines because I had been a hoodlum in civilian life. That carried over for my first few years in the service. I hung around the worst marines I could find because I considered myself just like them. I didn't look or act like a marine. I was lucky when I was assigned to Great Lakes. I met good marines there. I've finally started to grow up. Now, sir, I feel like and I'm trying to be a great marine."

"That's quite a story, marine. You sure look and carry yourself like a marine."

"Thank you, sir."

Franz made small talk with the other two officers and the Captain. Franz tried to remember all their mannerisms and ways of speech. He knew he looked sharper and more like a marine than all three of these officers. In the eyes of the other military personnel on the train, Franz looked like just another jarhead marine. He fit right in.

The train stopped in Tucson. The marines got off to stretch their legs, buy papers, and have a beer. One of the young second lieutenants brushed up against an oil-rig worker, a real roughneck who pushed the Officer back and said, "Get the hell out of my way, boy."

The young Officer, M. E. Gray, said, "Excuse me, sir."

The roughneck pushed him again. "So you're a badass marine, are you, boy?"

Lieutenant Gray's friend, the other marine second Lieutenant Bob Jolly, said, "Come on, M. E., let's go. These guys are drunk."

At that point, six roughnecks were surrounding the two officers.

The Captain walked over. "All right, let's break this up. You men go about your business."

One roughneck punched the Captain in the jaw, and he went down. The other roughnecks started hitting the lieutenants. Franz ran over and kicked one in back of his knee. As the man fell, Franz grabbed his hair, pulled his head back, and hit him in the nose. The man screamed. Before he hit the ground, Franz had kicked another in the groin and in the jaw. He grabbed a third by the collar, jerked his head down, and head-butted him in the jaw, breaking it and knocking him out. The remaining three roughnecks realized this one marine was beating the hell out of them. They turned on Franz but too late. Franz punched one in the throat and sent him to the ground. The remaining two put their hands up and backed off. The Captain had watched all this happen while he was on the ground.

The second lieutenants helped the Captain up and dusted him off. Lieutenant Gray said, "Did you see that, Captain Barious? He walked right through those men."

"I saw it, men. Damn. What a marine."

"Where did you learn to do that?" Lieutenant Jolly asked Franz.

"Good marine training sir."

"All aboard."

"Let's go, men," the Captain said.

As the marines ran to the train, other military men patted Franz on the back. *No big deal. If you had had to deal with drunks in all the bars and clubs I've been in, you could have done the same.* Franz was beginning to feel like a marine and was being treated like one.

In San Diego, Franz signed in and received his orders to board a ship heading to China, a voyage of about two weeks. He had always liked the smell and the quiet of the ocean. The voyage was uneventful. Franz stored in his head everything he could learn about the military and how military men acted and carried themselves. The Captain and the second lieutenants were onboard but in officers' quarters. Franz was able to sew on lance Corporal stripes. He wrote to Miss Mattie Blue, whose dad worked for Daddy Rabbit. He used the name Matt Summers, and he always called her Miss Mattie. The letters were really for Suzie Davis. Daddy Rabbit made sure she got them. Suzie would write back using the name of Mattie Blue. Suzie sent Franz pictures of herself on the Indian with Daddy Rabbit at the helm. She sent pictures of herself at a party. Franz told her of his voyage and of the men he had palled up with. He talked of the poker he got into aboard ship. He told her marines would bet on anything.

He met men who painted and men who whittled. Many had musical instruments they played, and others tried to sing. The Colonel of the marines onboard set up a target range to qualify his men in firearms. Franz scored expert marksman with the army Colt .45 automatic, the marine-issue M-1 Garand rifle, and the M-1903 Springfield rifle. Franz surprised everyone with his ability to fire expert on the Thompson. He earned the reputation of being one of the finest marines aboard.

Captain Barious asked the Colonel of the division if he would assign Lance Corporal Summers to him as his driver and aide. The Captain told the Colonel, "We have a history. I trust this marine." The Colonel agreed. The paperwork went through.

Franz passed some of his time showing marines how to fight with a knife—not the stand-up fighting taught by the corps but street fighting, the kind to kill someone. He helped some men work on their clothing to make them look sharper. The ship had a laundry and a sewing machine, so Franz showed these men how to tailor their uniforms to fit.

During the two weeks onboard, Franz became the kindly old uncle with all the right advice. He told the men about the history of China and of the first and the current Sino-Japanese war. He told them the history of the Chinese Communists and the Chinese Nationalists. He liked sharing his knowledge with the younger troops, and he gained the respect of most of the men onboard.

Franz alerted the Captain as to which marines were cheating when they gambled. Some were good, but most were sloppy. Franz had seen it all and was expert at catching cheats. He knew that when cheats were caught—and most of them would be—they would maybe be thrown overboard or worse.

The ship landed at Fuzhoa, a new port in China. The Nationalist Army still occupied this city in strength. The Communist Army wanted to take the city but could not; there were too many Japanese close by who would join the fight if the Communists tried to take Fuzhoa. Europeans and Americans were pouring into Fuzhoa from Shanghai. They did not care who won the war; they figured that if they just hung around and stayed neural, they would end up on the winning side. But that was getting harder to do with the war raging in Europe. It was just a matter of time before it spilled over into the China Sea.

Many government employees were sending their families to neutral countries and to the United States. Businessmen were doing the same with their families. At the time, Fuzhoa was as safe as any place. The new marine division was moving in to protect American interests and American families. These new China marines had to be sharp and ready for anything. Being a China marine used to be one of the better assignments. China had plenty of everything and was an inexpensive place to live. Even the men in the lowest ranks could live like kings there. Many of them retired in China because they were not allowed to bring their Chinese wives and children to America.

Fuzhoa was an exciting modern city; commerce there was bustling. The marines landed and moved into their new home, a small, old

Chinese army post that was falling down. The barracks housed only half the Marines, and there was no place to park all their vehicles. It was in a part of town surrounded by Americans and Europeans.

The Colonel of the marines called his officers together to discuss evacuating the area, which would have been hard to defend—too many troops and no room to maneuver. The best the marines could do was get the Americans out of the city to safer places.

The Colonel told Captain Barious to scout a site on high ground outside the city that they would be able to defend. "We'll have to protect a couple thousand civilians if and when the time comes. Pick a place we can escape from if we have to. We'll leave a company of forty men and equipment in the old post and move everybody else to the new site. I want it done now, marine."

"Aye aye sir," the Captain said as he saluted.

Captain Barious called for his truck. Franz drove it over with two other marines in the back. The Captain said, "Marines, we're going on a little scouting trip. I want you fully armed and ready for anything."

The marines scouted the area all day and finally found and old horse-racing track on a hill by the marshland near the coast. The property was large enough and close enough to the Americans in case they had to walk to it. It had some repairable buildings and a large parking area. The Captain said, "Welcome home, marines. This is our new camp."

Captain Barious told the Colonel about the racetrack, and he thought it was exactly what he wanted. The marines had to repair the buildings there and build a chow hall and showers. They built a tent city in the track's infield. The officers got single rooms in the old stalls. They built walkways and machine-gun posts on top of the buildings. They had to create a motor pool and storage areas. Colonel Adams assigned a hundred marines and hired a hundred coolies to handle the work. He wanted the roads from the city to the track smoothed and repaired. He also wanted the marsh hand-dug out to let small motorboats operate.

The Colonel gave Captain Barious the whole assignment and gave him a new second Lieutenant, Petey Amundus, an engineer just out of

Officer candidate school. The Lieutenant's dad, a full Colonel in the Marines, wanted his son to be one as well.

Lieutenant Amundus was not a very good marine; he had not wanted to join, but the day after he graduated from NYU with a degree in fashion design, his dad signed him up in the Marines. His dad had pull enough to get his son into the engineers. His dad was under the mistaken idea that if his son became a marine, he would start liking females. He did not believe his son could be a jeep—a homosexual—and a marine at the same time. He thought it was the result of the boy's mother letting him play with paper dolls and showing him how to sew. His mother had tea-partied with him as a child and let him sleep with a teddy bear. He took some of the blame himself being in the Marines and away from home much of the time. He had not been there enough to make sure his boy learned all the boy stuff he had to learn to be a real man.

His wife had graduated from NYU and was a home ec teacher. All she knew was women's and home stuff; he was sure that was why his boy was a homosexual rather than a tough man. He wanted the Marines to teach his boy how to become one. The China marines were some of the best, and he had known some of the division officers for years. They knew they would be good for his boy. His boy's new Commander was Colonel Marcus Adams, an old classmate of his from the Naval Academy with whom he had remained good friends.

Colonel Adams called Captain Barious in. "Captain, you're my best Officer. I want you to take over the training of our new second Lieutenant. He's the son of one of my closest friends. I want you to make a marine out of him. His personnel records look pretty bleak. It makes him look like a bad marine. I think it's because no one has taken the time to work with him. Do you understand me, Captain?"

"Aye aye sir" Captain Barious said. *This means I have to babysit a spoiled brat whose dad has some pull. He'll be looking over my shoulder every time I make him cry. This is all I need.*

"Corporal Summers, report to me now."

"Aye aye sir. Corporal Summers reporting sir," Franz said.

"Matt, I have an assignment for you. Lieutenant Amundus is new, and he needs an old marine like you to take him under his wing and show him how to be as sharp as you are. He has connections to our Colonel, and his dad is a full Colonel too. Take care of this for me, Matt."

"Aye aye sir, will do." Franz saluted and walked away. *Why did I get stuck with this loser? I'm trying to keep a low profile and now I have to babysit some brass's kid.*

Franz walked to the day room, where he was told the new Lieutenant was waiting for him. Franz walker up to the Lieutenant, came to attention, and saluted. The new Lieutenant was surprised. He finally returned the salute so Franz could drop his hand. Franz stuck out his hand. "Sir, I'm Lance Corporal Matt Summers. I'm your new aide."

The Lieutenant took Franz's hand weakly. "I'm Petey Amundus. Sorry. Second Lieutenant Petus Amundus."

Franz could see that this boy was just like the real Matt Summers. He did not want to be a marine or be where he was. He was a disgrace to his uniform, which was not pressed or clean. It fit him like a cheap suit. His hair was too long, and his teeth were not brushed. Franz knew he was a homosexual as soon as he met him. Franz did not care one way or the other about the man's sexual preferences. He had known plenty in the businesses he had been in. He could tell by the way the sad sack presented himself that his job of straightening him out would be very hard.

"Sir, are you checked in? Have they given you a place to sleep?"

"Yes, Corporal. I'm assigned to the officers' quarters, room a-sixteen. I'm going there now."

Franz picked up the Lieutenant's duffel bag. "Sir, if you'll follow me, I'll take you there."

"Yes sir."

"Lieutenant, you don't call me sir. You call me Corporal or Matt."

"Okay. It will be Matt or marine."

Franz took him to his room, a converted horse stall with a wood floor and a single rack—a bed in marine parlance—and a wall locker and bookshelves. An oil lamp hung from a wire. The door was a set of curtains. Outside the room in the hallway were wood stoves and piles of wood about every twenty feet.

"Lieutenant, the head is outside to the right. It has sinks, American toilets, showers, and sometimes hot water." Franz could see that the Lieutenant was about ready to cry. *Is this beneath him? The enlisted men living in eight-man tents would love this.*

Some of the top NCOs also lived in the stables. All the men had Chinese maids who did their cleaning and laundry. The one chow hall was staffed mostly by Chinese under American supervision. Franz would go into the chow hall at least once a week and make a dinner for the Colonel and his staff and the officers he worked for. Some of the men, who had been stationed all over the world, told Franz his Swiss food was the best they had ever had and that he should be the chef for a General or Admiral. Franz would laugh and say that he was waiting for Colonel Adams to be promoted and then he would be. And they would all laugh.

Franz took Petey to the tailor in town and had his uniforms tailored to fit. He took him to the barber for a shave and a haircut. He hired a maid for Petey and showed her how he wanted the Lieutenant's uniforms washed, starched, and ironed. Franz showed the maid how to keep the Lieutenant's room spotless.

The only reason the Lieutenant let Franz do all this was because Franz had told him he would get him, the Captain, and the other two enlisted men in trouble if he did not. They would get busted and would not be able to support their families. He knew the Lieutenant had a soft heart.

Franz took the Lieutenant and the other two marines to the shooting range. The Lieutenant carried a Colt .45 automatic and was allowed to carry a Thompson, but Franz carried it most of the time. The Lieutenant began to get used to the noise and was getting better with his .45. *The Lieutenant will get the hang of everything by the time he retires. Did I give my dad this much trouble? Probably. Now I'm being punished for it. I did all my shenanigans because I was depressed and mean. This kid is doing it because he feels depressed and ashamed.*

Franz finally got a letter from Leslie. He used Franz's new name, but he could write his letters without using code, and Franz could write back without using code. Leslie sent pictures of Suzie. They kept making plans to meet each other but could not get it worked out. Leslie told Franz of his plan to get out of the military, marry Irani, and live in Hawaii as a welder just as Alma and Woodley had done. Franz told him that when he got set up in Hawaii to let Suzie Davis know and she could come to Hawaii. Leslie wrote Franz about the cranes he had seen and how they made the world seem a better place. Franz got to where he looked for them too. His Lieutenant began to like the cranes also.

Franz helped the Lieutenant built the gun emplacements around the camp, and they built escape routes and tunnels. The American sector kept getting bigger and more crowded. If anything happened, half the American would perish before they could be evacuated.

The US president finally told the American companies operating in China that they had to send their people to Hawaii, Australia, or the Philippines because the US forces in China could not protect them. The president also ordered the US diplomatic corps out of China. Gunboats and other ships started ferrying Americans out. The military was ordered to take their white families to safety as well. There was no panic, but the military knew it would start as soon as the Japanese started shelling Fuzhoa.

Franz was ordered to take a squad of men under Lieutenant Amundus and start rounding up Americans who lived outside the city. They took a utility vehicle and a truck and headed west to a Catholic mission twenty miles outside the city. The Lieutenant and a driver rode in the front of the utility car. Franz sat in the back with a Thompson. Three more men followed them in the truck.

When the convoy got to the mission, the priest told the Lieutenant he and the other priest and the nuns would not be leaving the mission. They and three American couples wanted to take care of the sixty orphans there. The Lieutenant told the priest he had orders to bring everyone at the mission to Fuzhoa so they could board a ship out of China. The priests and the nuns refused to leave. The Lieutenant told the three American couples to pack up, they were leaving. The three couples offered little argument. The priest told them it was okay to leave. The couples—teachers and one doctor—told the priest they would be back as soon as the scare was over.

Halfway back to Fuzhoa, the convoy ran into a checkpoint manned by a Japanese Officer and four enlisted men. The Japanese ordered everyone out of the vehicles and ordered the marines to lay down their weapons. The Lieutenant motioned for the marines to do as the Japanese Officer had told them. The Officer separated the Americans into three groups—the four marine Privates, the Lieutenant and Franz, and the three couples. He ordered everyone to empty pockets and take off jewelry and watches. He had one of his men pick up all the wallets, jewelry, watches, and anything else of value. He told one of his men to put the marines' weapons in his truck.

Franz could tell that the Japanese had been drinking and that it was just a cheap holdup. The Japanese Officer grabbed one of the women and made her get to her knees. He grabbed her hair and rubbed her face in his crouch. He laughed and slapped her and grabbed one of the other women. All the Japanese soldiers were laughing.

The Lieutenant was shaking badly. Franz could see fear in his eyes. When the Lieutenant tried to help the first woman up, the Officer hit him and sent him to the ground. The Lieutenant had been hit in his face but was holding his stomach. Franz figured he was going to throw up. He was afraid that might encourage the Japanese to really start abusing them.

Franz had palmed his hawk-billed knife and had it in his hand. He slowly opened it and took a fast step. He slashed the throats of the two closest Japanese soldiers in one quick motion. It happened so fast that the Officer did not see it. Franz grabbed the Officer's throat and his sidearm. The marines grabbed the other two Japanese as they were struggling to react; they disarmed them.

Franz hollered to the marines to move the bodies to the side of the road and retrieve their weapons and personal stuff. He told the civilians to retrieve their stuff and get back in the truck. Franz helped the Lieutenant up and walked him to the back of the utility car so no one could see exactly where the Lieutenant had gotten sick from fear.

Franz shouted to the marines that the Lieutenant wanted them to put the Japanese into their truck, put the dead Officer in the cab and the two live ones in the bed and watch them. "The Lieutenant said to put all the roadblock into the back of the Japanese truck. Start the Japanese truck and cut one of the front tires. Try to make it look like it was done by a sharp rock. Pour gasoline all over the front and back of the truck. Find their sake bottles and open them. Put the truck in gear, and let me in the back."

Franz jumped on the back of the Japanese truck and hit one of the soldiers in the face with a road-paving stone, which knocked him cold. Franz grabbed the other soldier and broke his arms. That made a marine throw up. "Light this Japanese Roman candle up."

A marine set the Japanese truck on fire. They heard the Japanese soldier with the broken arms screaming. He and the last soldier jumped off the truck completely on fire and died on the road.

"The Lieutenant wants to talk to me about this," Franz told the marines. "All of you ride in the truck with the civilians." The Lieutenant had not said a word since he had been knocked to the ground; Franz was just saying the Lieutenant had given orders to protect the Lieutenant. Franz made sure no one saw Lieutenant Amundus in bad shape. Franz knew he would never be a marine. He felt sorry for him.

On the trip back to Fuzhoa, Franz explained what had happened at the roadblock and what he had done that the Lieutenant had supposedly ordered.

"Thank you. I really appreciate your trying to help me, but I think I'm hopeless," the Lieutenant said. He broke into tears.

If we were stateside or if we weren't facing a war, I'd cover for you and make sure your secrets were kept quiet. "Lieutenant, I'm going to have to figure out what to do about you. You're a good kid, but you do not need to be a marine."

"Matt, I'm too scared to go to sleep. Would you stay with me tonight in my office? I just don't think I could be alone. I think I might hurt myself."

"Sure, Lieutenant, I can do that." *All I need is for him to hurt himself and for his father to blame me. I'd get investigated and kicked out of the Marines and sent to the brig.*

It was after dark when the convoy pulled into the post. Franz said, "The Lieutenant wants you civilians to go to that office over there." Franz pointed to the visitors' center. "The Lieutenant wants each of you men to write down what happened on the road today while it's still fresh in your mind and turn them in to me." Franz wanted to see what they wrote down so he could adjust it to protect the Lieutenant. He wanted to know if anyone had seen the Lieutenant throw up or cry.

When the Lieutenant and Franz got to the Lieutenant's office, the Lieutenant asked him to explain what he had done and how he had known to do it. "I knew we had to take care of the Japanese. They were drunk. They were going to rob us, rape the women, and kill us. I decided I had to act. I burned up everything so it would look like the Japanese soldiers were drunk, had hit something in the road and blown out a tire, which caused the truck to wreck and catch on fire. It's all I could figure to do, but Lieutenant, the men and the civilians think it was all your idea. I suggest you let everyone keep thinking that."

Doyle had taught him and Daddy Rabbit to do that in Miami. Two New Jersey gangsters had tried to move in on the gambling near the club Isaiah Green ran. The two came into the club and told Isaiah they were to receive a cut on all gambling in his club. Isaiah told them to get lost. One of the men hit him in the stomach, making Isaiah bend over.

Doyle rushed over to Isaiah, but one of the men put a gun in Doyle's face. "Where the hell do you think you're going, Grampaw?" They pushed Doyle to the floor.

Franz had been out of town that day collecting. He got to the club about midnight and heard about the New Jersey gangsters. Doyle made some calls to some of his old police buddies and found out where the gangsters were staying, a rooming house at 587 South West Twenty-Ninth. When Doyle picked up the boys the next day at noon, he had an old bicycle in the car.

"Doyle, you going to start riding a bike?"

Doyle laughed. "No. We need this for later." Franz and Isaiah looked at each other and shrugged.

That evening about eleven, Doyle told the boys he had to run an errand but would be back. Within thirty minutes, Doyle came back to the club and told Franz to come with him. He told Isaiah they would be back in a hour.

Doyle drove to where the men were staying and pointed it out. "They're here. I just checked on them. This is what we're going to do." Doyle told Franz the plan. They got out of the car. Doyle picked up a brick. They knocked on the door. When one of the men opened it, Doyle hit him in the face with the brick and knocked him out. Franz rushed in and put a gun in the other man's face. They told him to pick up his friend and take him to their car. While his was putting his friend in their car, Franz holding a gun on them, Doyle went into their room and gathered two scotch bottles, one empty and the other half full. He came out to the car and poured some of the scotch on both men.

Doyle had Franz break the previously unhurt man's arms and put him in the car. They started the engine. Doyle poured gasoline in the car and on the men. He told Franz to gun the engine and let the car speed down the driveway when he said so.

Doyle took the bicycle to the end of the drive. He waved to Franz. Franz sent the car speeding down the driveway. Just before it got to Doyle, he pushed the bike in front of the car. The car hit the bike. Doyle lit the gasoline. Both men jumped out of the car on fire and screaming. They died in the street.

The police report said the two men had been drunk and had hit a bicycle that caused their car to wreck and catch on fire. The two men were able to get out of the car but too late. They died at the scene of the accident.

That had worked in Miami. Franz figured it would work in rural China.

The following morning, Franz collected the reports the men had written. They had not seen the Lieutenant throw up or cry. They all thought the Lieutenant had given all the orders. Franz wrote his and the Lieutenant's reports and had the Lieutenant sign his.

Captain Barious read the reports. "Corporal, this sounds like some of your handiwork, not that pansy's. But you won't tell me, will you?"

Franz just smiled.

"Marine, don't you have some babysitting to do?"

Franz saluted and left for chow.

For the next two weeks, they went out to bring American civilians to safety and had no problems. On the twelfth rescue trip, they ran into the Japanese again, two officers and two enlisted men. One Officer spoke very good English. They were investigating the wreck and deaths of their five men. Franz told them he did not know anything about any Japanese in any wreck. Franz could feel the Lieutenant shaking as they sat in their vehicle. He knew the Lieutenant would spill everything if they scared him enough. He was sure the Japanese had also seen the Lieutenant shaking.

When they got back, Franz told the Captain of their meeting with the Japanese and that their men needed some time off. The Captain told Franz to tell the Lieutenant he and his men had three-day passes.

Franz, the Lieutenant, and the squad took off for a vacation to Fuzhoa. Franz wanted to buy some silk for Suzie and Brigitta. He would send it to Mattie Blue to give to them. The first place he and the Lieutenant went was to a garden party held at the British envoy's home. The Lieutenant had been invited, and he took Franz as his aide. Franz was in his best dress uniform and was having a good time. He danced and ate and told stories of his travels to a number of British women. He made his travel stories seem as if he had traveled while in the Marines. He pretended to be a European aristocrat; his German accent seemed to back that up. He was one of the hits of the party.

Franz kept imagining himself with Suzie at this party. Franz strolled the grounds daydreaming about dancing with Suzie there when he heard his Lieutenant sobbing. The sound was coming from a cabana. He stayed outside and heard someone with a British accent calmly and gently talking to the Lieutenant. "Now Petey, my love, it's going to be okay. As soon as the Japanese attack, I'll take you to South Africa with me. You'll never have to be a marine again."

Franz peeked into the cabana and saw the two men naked and in bed with each other. He backed away. Franz felt sorry for the Lieutenant.

Later that evening, Franz was introduced to the British diplomat who had been in bed with the Lieutenant. He introduced Franz to his wife and son. Franz made small talk with the diplomat and his family for a while. He told them he had to see someone.

The next two days were relaxing for Franz. He and the Lieutenant toured the harbor and the shopping district, gambled at some casinos, and ate at a French restaurant and an Argentine steak house. The Lieutenant spent the nights with his British diplomat.

On the bus back to camp, Franz said, "Let's get off the bus a couple of miles from the camp so we can talk."

The Lieutenant agreed. He and Franz got out four miles from camp. "Lieutenant, I'm your friend and your aide. I think of you as a younger brother. I feel I need to protect you and train you for life, not just the Marines."

"What do you mean?"

"Lieutenant, I know about your relationship with that Brit."

"Oh no! You're not going to tell my father, are you?"

"No, Lieutenant. I'm not going to tell anyone. It's no one's business with whom you have a relationship. But I need to talk to you about it. I know the diplomat wants you to go away with him. Sir, do you know he's married and has children?"

"Yes."

"Sir, he's not going to leave his wife and children for you. He wants you to be his Saturday night boy. He'll keep you in an apartment somewhere and never take you out in public because of his wife and children. As soon as he gets tired of you, you'll find yourself on the streets, and by then you'll be a deserter. You'll never get to go home. If the Marines catch you, you'll probably get shot. Sir, I know you're lonely. So am I. My lady love is back in the states. I haven't seen her in six months.

"Sir, we need to find a hobby for both of us, something to keep our minds occupied. Sir, I'm here for you. Anytime you need to talk, find me. I'll be all ears, and I know how to keep my mouth shut."

The Lieutenant shook his head and started crying again.

Damn. He's got to quit crying. Someone is going to see him one of these days.

CHAPTER 13

Hopeless

Franz noticed a stray dog following them. It should have weighed seventy-five pounds but was a skinny forty-five pounds. Franz could count his bones through his skin. His tail was making a ninety-degree turn. It had been beaten before. One of his dewclaws was bleeding and infected. Franz could see ticks and fleas all over the mutt.

"Lieutenant, let's adopt this dog. He needs a home, and we need a hobby—training this dog."

The Lieutenant looked at the dog and smiled. "Do you think we can keep him? Do you think he has a master?"

"No sir. I think he is as lonely as we are. We can keep him."

They led the dog to camp. They sprayed him with DDT powder to kill the ticks and fleas. The dog was such a sad sack that the Lieutenant asked if they could name him Hopeless and call him Hope.

That's a pansy name for a dog, but why not? This will give the Lieutenant something to occupy his time and maybe keep him out of trouble. "Sure," Franz replied. "Sounds like a great name to me."

"Let's take him to the doctor and have him checked out," the Lieutenant said.

Franz saw the Lieutenant upbeat and smiling for the first time.

They took Hopeless to the camp doctor, who said, "I'm an MD, not a vet. Anyway, this dog is not going to live very long."

"Why?" asked the Lieutenant. "What's wrong with him?"

"To start with, he's eaten up with worms and has an infection in his leg from the trauma to his dewclaw. He's beyond skinny. His tail is going to get infected too."

"What do we need to do?" the Lieutenant asked.

Franz asked the doctor if he could do all the medical stuff the dog needed. He told him that he knew it wasn't a job for a doctor but that they really wanted to help the dog. He said they could not pay the doctor but maybe could trade for the work. Franz asked the doctor if there was anything the doctor wanted or needed.

The doctor thought for a minute. "I'd have to cut most of the tail off. I could leave him about five inches. I'd have to remove his dewclaws, and I could give him the same worm medicine I give some of the marines. If that doesn't kill him, you'll have to put some weight on him. This dog should be over seventy pounds."

Hopeless, who had short, black-and-white fur and one brown and one black eye, looked much better after his operations and a good bath. The Lieutenant brushed Hopeless's teeth and combed him. He was actually a good-looking dog. He followed the Lieutenant everywhere, including rescue assignments in the countryside. Franz was surprised at the Lieutenant's change in attitude. The dog slept in the Lieutenant's bed with him. The Lieutenant had a leash and collar made for Hopeless out of a marine belt.

The Lieutenant's father was happy to read good, upbeat letters from his son. He wrote to Colonel Adams about how pleased he was that the Colonel was helping train his son. The Colonel was so pleased he called in Captain Barious to express his gratitude. Then the Captain called in Franz to let him know he and the Colonel were so pleased that they had put Franz in for a promotion to full Corporal and a pay grade of E-4.

Franz was well pleased with himself. He had been promoted and had gained the respect of all the men around him. He has less than a year left in the Marines. He could then go home to marry Suzie and start a family. He had been buying two twenty-five-dollar savings bonds every month on payday. He mailed them in the name of Matt Summers to Mattie Blue, who gave them to Suzie Davis.

Franz played a little poker for money but made sure he did not win more than ten or so dollars a week. He did not want to bust any of his marine buddies or be accused of cheating. He also gave poker lessons to some of the marines; he taught them how to bet and when to bet and when to fold.

The Lieutenant taught Franz how to play chess, and he was becoming very good at it. Chess was the kind of game Franz liked; he had to think ahead in the game and outthink the opponent.

The Captain was sending the Lieutenant and his men, including Franz, to Fu'an, a city north of Fuzhoa. They were to help an American businessman pack up his valuables and family and bring them to Fuzhoa to board a ship to Hawaii. The Captain told the Lieutenant to make sure they took the big truck.

Two marines were in the truck, and the Lieutenant and Franz were in the utility car that left that morning. Hopeless was in the backseat. The trip was very slow. The roads were thronged with people heading south.

The convoy stopped for the night. The men slept in the back of the truck and let Hopeless stand guard. He was a good guard dog.

The next morning, the convoy made it to the American and his family in Fu'an. They spent the day packing the man and his family's belongings up and getting it all on the truck. The man had two sons and a daughter. One son was married. He and his wife had a child.

They started south at dawn the next day. The convoy had to add the man's cars so everyone could make the trip. The utility car led, followed by the man's chauffeured limousine carrying the businessman and his wife and a son and the daughter. Another car was driven by the other son and held his wife and baby and the nanny. The cargo truck with two marines and a butler brought up the rear.

The trip took two days. By the time they got into camp, Franz thought he was going to kill the stuck-up businessman and his horrible wife. She had to stop for tea every four hours and then to stop so she could relieve herself. They had to unload the truck so she could have a bed put in it at night for her to sleep on. She had to have the nanny fix her meals, which had to be served on the good china. On top of that, the couple's married son apologized for his parents about every hour for two days.

The Captain met them as they were unloading the truck. He told them to go back to Fu'an for a French diplomat and his family. The marines ate and got a good night's sleep. They started back that morning, drove hard, and got to Fu'an in a day.

The French diplomat was also a stuffed shirt, but his family was very nice as well as scared and happy to leave China. They had packed only their clothes and their most-prized belongings. The French diplomat, his wife, and their four children were going to Canada.

Everybody fit into the two vehicles. The convoy left early the next morning. They got to the outskirts of town and stopped when they saw an elderly couple by a car whose radiator was steaming. This couple had been driving to Fuzhoa. They asked the Lieutenant to take them. The Lieutenant looked at Franz, who nodded. The couple hopped in the back of the truck.

At the first break in the driving, the passengers got out for bathroom breaks. The passengers changed seats. The diplomat's wife decided to ride in the cab of the truck with her youngest daughter. One son rode in the utility car with Hopeless and played with the dog the rest of the day.

The road was hot, dusty, and crowded. The trip would take two days at the rate they were going on the crowded road. They stopped for the night and set up camp. The marines had C rations for everyone. The younger children loved the food, but the adults complained about it and wanted wine. The marines had coffee. The children and the women slept in the back of the truck, the men on the ground. Hopeless walked circles around the group keeping guard, something he had not been taught to do, but guard duty seemed to come naturally to him. When Hopeless slept, it was beside the Lieutenant, who would sleep with his arms around Hopeless. Franz thought, *He just needed someone to love and someone to love him.*

The convoy got to Fuzhoa about fourteen hundred hours the next day. The Lieutenant told everyone to take the next day off. He said he would round them up when he needed them.

Two days later, the Captain sent word to the Lieutenant. They were going to Fu'an again for another family. The doctor sent word that he needed to talk to Franz. He showed Franz some red and green jade jewelry and some red and green jade figurines. He showed Franz how to spot the good stuff from the average stuff. He told Franz to remember their deal. Franz and the Lieutenant were to buy as much of the best jade as they could in Fu'an. The doctor had learned many Europeans leaving Fu'an were selling their jade there to raise cash. The doctor told Franz he was sending jade home for his retirement.

"Why not? I'll get you what I can find. A deal's a deal," Franz said.

He told the Lieutenant about his talk with the doctor and what they had to do. The Lieutenant agreed.

On the trip to Fu'an, the convoy was stopped by a Japanese roadblock. These Japanese were sober and threatening. They held up the convoy for two hours going through the utility car and the truck. The Japanese told the marines that they were closing Fu'an to all foreigners and that they needed to get in and out fast. The marines knew to be nice and friendly with the Japanese, to thank them, and to do what they had told them to do.

The Lieutenant got to the American civilians and told them the Japanese would close the city. He told them to tell all the remaining Americans to get out. The Americans who were married to Chinese women told Franz they were going inland about a thousand miles, where they felt they would be safe. Franz agreed that they needed to get out of Fu'an but had no idea were safe was.

The marines loaded the eight Americans and their luggage on the truck. The Lieutenant told Franz that he had told an American he and his family could follow them in their car. The Lieutenant asked Franz if they had the time to look for jade for the doctor. Franz said no.

As they left Fu'an, Franz noticed that there were six carloads of people following them. *Damn.*

They got to the roadblock. The Japanese stopped them. The Japanese Officer recognized them. "Are you carrying anything of value?"

"No, only personal belongings," Franz said.

The Japanese Officer waved them through without looking at anything. Franz motioned the convoy to follow him and the Lieutenant.

Halfway to Fuzhoa, the convoy stopped for the night. They pulled into an old, run-down farm with a couple of mudbrick buildings with intact roofs. One marine who had been brought up on a farm collected root vegetables, wild tomatoes, hot peppers, and some fruit. The other marine helped the women make a place for themselves in one of the huts. The twelve civilian men stayed in the other hut. The marines and the dog were going to stay in the back of the truck. The Lieutenant told his marines to unpack the C rations from the Great War, the same food they had had to endure on the last trip.

Franz told the Lieutenant to let him prepare the evening meal. The Lieutenant said, "Can I help? I just love to cook."

"Sure," Franz said. "Lieutenant, I'll show you how to make haute cuisine out of C rations."

One of the women said that she would like to help, that it would help pass the time and keep her from thinking how scared she was.

Franz and his sous-chefs boiled some vegetables and fried others, mixing the meat bouillon with them. The C rations came with salt, pepper, and sugar, so they had some seasoning besides the hot peppers.

Franz chopped up the fruit and poured some sugar and water on it to make a Chinese version of a fruit cocktail. The meal was quite good; at least it was not C rations. The Lieutenant and the marines were shocked that this hard-ass marine who had cut the throats of Japanese soldiers, shot one, and burned alive two could cook like a European chef. The civilians actually thought he was from the mess hall.

Late that night, Franz and the dog decided they had to take a pee. They walked to the back of the farm and relieved themselves. Franz chuckled. *This dog even knows how to pee like a marine.*

On the way back to the farm, Franz saw three Japanese trucks and a utility vehicle pull up. Franz saw nine drunk and loud Japanese soldiers, no Officer, only one Sergeant. They were unkempt, undisciplined, and looking for trouble. They rounded up the civilians and the marines into two groups according to sex. Four stood guard while the rest went through the luggage. They put the rest of the food into a truck and loaded the marines' weapons in their utility vehicle.

Franz knew these Japanese were conscripts, not professional soldiers. They would kill the men and rape the women if they could. They constituted a mob, not a military force.

One soldier went to the woods and squatted to defecate. Franz cut his throat. As the man slumped, Hopeless lifted a leg on him. Franz took the soldier's weapon and hid it near their truck. Franz slid under the marine truck and grabbed another Japanese soldier. He stabbed him and pulled him under the truck, hiding his weapon as well. Franz wanted to find the Lieutenant. Franz patted the dog and whispered, "Go find Petey, boy."

Hopeless ran down to the ditch across the road and stood. Franz crawled to the ditch, where the Lieutenant was quietly crying and shaking so badly that Franz thought someone would hear his teeth chattering.

The Lieutenant turned to Franz. "Let's get out of here. There's nothing we can do for them. Take me out of here."

Franz patted his back. "Just be quiet. I'll come back for you soon." He slid back across the road to the farm and saw one Japanese soldier looking for the first one he had killed. Franz told Hopeless to stay behind the truck. He crept up behind the man, pulled him in with one hand, and slashed his throat. The man was dead before he hit the ground.

Franz tied a piece of cord to the soldier's rifle and Hopeless's collar. He patted Hopeless and told him to go to Greg, a marine who sometimes played with Hopeless. The dog walked over to Greg, pulling the rifle. A Japanese soldier saw him but did not pay any attention. Stray dogs were common. Greg saw the rifle and untied it from Hopeless's collar, and he and the other marine hid it under themselves.

The Japanese soldiers were getting rough on the women, who were crying and screaming. The soldiers laughed and grabbed them to make them squeal more. One soldier was taking a drunken nap in one of their trucks. Franz snuck up, slipped a wire around his neck, and choked him to death. The other soldiers were having so much fun that they did not notice four of their comrades were not moving. Franz put on a Japanese helmet and held his head down as he walked to where the men were being guarded by one drunken soldier. He stabbed the Japanese in the kidney and killed him. He let the soldier slide down as if were sitting down. Greg took the soldier's weapon and gave it to the other marine.

Franz whispered, "The Lieutenant says that when he gives the order, cut those four men down. No Japanese is to live."

The marines nodded.

Franz went to the ditch the Lieutenant was hiding in. He saw the Lieutenant on his stomach with his head covered. Franz aimed at him with a Japanese weapon and pulled the trigger. The marines shot the four Japanese soldiers to pieces. The Lieutenant screamed. Franz fired a couple more times before he fired his own weapon. Franz hollered, "Everything okay? Anyone hurt?"

"No, Corporal," Greg said. "We killed four Japanese. Everybody here's okay."

"The Lieutenant has been hit. He's going to live, but his kneecap is gone."

Franz had his men drive the Japanese trucks to the marsh and put the Japanese bodies under the outhouse. He bandaged up the Lieutenant's leg and told him about the firefight. He told the Lieutenant to tell the story the way he was telling it to him.

"Which one of them shot me?" the Lieutenant asked.

Franz pointed to one. "That one."

The convoy packed up and was on the road before dawn. They got to Fuzhoa by twelve hundred hours with no more incidents. The Colonel asked Franz how the Lieutenant had gotten shot in the knee.

"Sir, there were nine of them. They were all around us in the camp at the farm. When the fighting started, one Jap just got off a lucky shot from behind us. I was able to get him before he could hit anyone else."

"Is that how you're going to write it up, marine?" asked the Colonel.

"Yes sir."

"That will get him out of the Marines in an honorable way. His dad will be proud of him. Corporal, that will also takes care of our problem with him. Good riddance."

"I'll miss him, sir," Franz said. "He was a good Officer to me." Franz smiled and walked away. He saw Hopeless, the real hero of the show, looking for a bone. Franz walked to the hospital with a burlap bag he had gotten out of one of the Japanese trucks. It contained five big, red jade figurines. He was taking it to the doctor. They would be even. He went over what he would tell the Lieutenant. *Lieutenant, I'm sorry I had to shoot you, but you were going to get us killed one day. You wanted to leave the men behind to be killed. Sir, I shot you to get you out of the Marines, not kill you. You'll get a small pension and can go live in New York and do your fashions. Good luck to you, sir.*

Franz got to the Lieutenant's room in the temporary hospital. The Captain was there. He told Franz, "The Lieutenant is now a first Lieutenant. His promotion came in while you guys were out in the field."

"Congratulations, Lieutenant," Franz said and saluted.

"Thank you, Matt," the Lieutenant said and stuck out his hand. Franz shook it. The Captain said his good-byes and left.

The Lieutenant kept hold of Franz's hand. "They're going to put me out of the Marines. I can't pass the physical with my leg. That Japanese shot off my kneecap. I don't know how I feel about getting out of the Marines. At one time, all I wanted was out. But now I feel I was becoming a good marine Officer. I looked and felt like an Officer."

No, you were not going to be a good Officer. You had to get out of the Marines. "Lieutenant, I'm sure going to miss you." Franz meant that.

"I love you, Matt. You've been my best friend. I feel closer to you than anybody. You have only a few months left in the Marines. I want you to come to New York and live with me when you get out. Will you, Matt?"

"Lieutenant, I'll certainly think about it," replied Franz, not meaning a word.

The Lieutenant asked Franz if he thought the Marines would let him take Hopeless back to the states with him.

"I don't think so, Lieutenant." *They won't let the men take their Chinese wives and children back, so I'm sure they won't let him take a dog. Besides, Hopeless is half mine. I want him to stay with me.* "I don't think they'll let you take him on the plane with you because of your injury, Lieutenant. Don't worry about Hopeless, sir. I'll take care of him. Now that you're leaving, he'll be my new best friend."

The Lieutenant kissed Franz's hand. "Thank you, Matt. From now on, call me Petey. Is it okay if we write to each other?"

"Sure, Petey, I'd love to hear from you. I'll let you know how Hopeless is doing and how your marines are faring. I'll get a picture of us all for you to take to the states."

"Thanks, Matt. I'll miss you most of all."

Petey was sedated most of the day, but he told everybody who would listen about how he and his men had killed the Japanese. He told everyone Franz was a European aristocrat who had had to flee Europe because of a duel when he was young.

Where the hell did he get a story like that? Franz wondered.

The next morning, a Boeing 314 Clipper, a huge, new seaplane, took off from Fuzhoa with fifty passengers including three wounded men, one of them the Lieutenant. The Clipper was headed to Hawaii and would stop at Midway Island for refueling.

Franz wrote to Leslie about Petey Amundus and how he had gotten shot and was being put out of the Marines for a stiff leg. He sent Leslie a picture of himself and Hopeless. He told Leslie about his plan to join him in Hawaii, that he and Suzie would open a restaurant featuring Swiss and French foods. Suzie was taking lessons from John Greene, and John had told her she was a natural.

He told Leslie to get together with his mother's cousins and look for a good restaurant to buy. He said maybe he and Leslie could buy a duplex on the beach together. He told Leslie he was making up German food in a Chinese style and some of it was quite good. He was trying to make sauerkraut using Chinese cabbages; he'd tried *bok choy, pak choi, baechu,* and *pekineais* and was looking around for mushroom suitable for German and French dishes. The *shiitake* mushrooms were not close enough to the European varieties; the one that seemed the closest in size and flavor was the *agaricus,* but the one he thought he could make new recipes from was the *enoki.*

He and Suzie would have to ship German and French wines and German beers to Hawaii because Chinese beer was horrible and Chinese wine tasted like lighter fluid. Leslie wrote back that he kind of liked Chinese rice beer. He wrote to Leslie about Ranakii Fatz, a strange army Private who was an expert with weapons.

At night, he cooked and wrote to Suzie a page or so a day and mail it every two weeks to Mattie. He wrote Leslie every two weeks and Otto every month by writing to Mrs. Bagwell at her school.

After a couple of slow months at the camp in Fuzhoa, the Captain asked Franz to take his squad with a new Lieutenant on a small gunboat upriver to Nanping. He was then to find vehicles and drive up about twenty miles or so to rescue some holy Joes and their families who thought they could be in extreme danger. Apparently, they had tried praying for a while and finally decided to pray to the god of the Marines. "Matt, you can take the dog if you want," the Captain said with a chuckle.

CHAPTER **14**

Lieutenant Wiggins

The next morning, Franz and five men showed up at the dock to meet the new Lieutenant, who looked like a marine—all spit and polish. He walked like a marine. He was about five ten with broad shoulders. He was in great shape. This was his first duty assignment out of Officer candidate school, and he meant for it to be the jump-start of a successful career in the Marines. Franz introduced himself to the Lieutenant and saluted. The Lieutenant saluted. "I'm Lieutenant William Wiggins." He did not offer to shake Franz's hand.

Franz told his men to load their supplies, including twenty five-gallon gas cans, to the boat. The Lieutenant asked Franz why he was taking gas on a gunboat.

"Sir, I figure when we get to Nanping, we can find some cars or trucks instead of hiking through the country."

"Where will we find these vehicles, Corporal?" snapped the Lieutenant.

"Sir, there are abandoned vehicles all over China that are out of gasoline. I figure I can find us a couple, maybe three. It will make our trip faster and safer."

The Lieutenant did not reply. He tried to look as if he were busy with some paperwork and walked away.

Boy, this is going to be a long trip with that stuck-up ass along.

The riverboat headed upriver. Franz and the dog walked all around the boat.

The Lieutenant asked, "Whose dog is this?"

"Mine, sir," Franz said.

"Why the hell is it on this boat?"

"The Captain told me to bring him."

"Why was that?"

"I think it's because he's good at smelling Japanese before we can see them, sir."

"Don't let him get in the way or I'll have him shot. Do you understand me, Corporal?" The Lieutenant was glaring at Franz.

"Yes sir." Franz saluted.

Franz and his marines stayed away from the Lieutenant. They did not want to give him an excuse to berate them in front of the sailors on the riverboat.

This Lieutenant strutted around the boat like the cock of the walk. He talked only to the officers onboard. He treated the boat's chief like a regular sailor. Franz did not consider that smart or professional.

Halfway up the river, the gunboat was fired upon from the left bank. The boat's Captain said that it was pirates, that the Japanese were on the right bank. The Lieutenant told his men to form two lines and face left. With his marines and the ship's marines, he had twelve in all. He ordered the front row to grab a knee and the second line to stand and fire at the riverbank. Franz ran up and told the men to scatter.

"What the hell you doing?" the Lieutenant screamed. "I ordered those men to that firing formation and to fire at the enemy. You told them to disobey a direct order! I'll have you put in chains for this! Get them back on this deck and re-form now, Corporal!"

The Captain of the ship walked between the Lieutenant and Franz. "Can I see you over here a minute, Lieutenant?"

The Lieutenant looked at the Captain with disgust. "Aye aye sir." He walked away from Franz.

The Captain told the Lieutenant that it was not a good idea to have the men stand that close to each other, that they made easier targets that way. They should spread out all over the ship so the enemy would waste ammunition and not hit as many of them. "This will give us time to pick off some."

"That's not what it says in the marine manual," replied the Lieutenant.

"I know," said the Captain, "but that's how it's done in the field. Let's not get any of our men killed. Do you understand me, Lieutenant?"

"Aye aye sir," said the Lieutenant in a condescending way.

"Dismissed!" the Captain saluted and walked away.

The Lieutenant saw the bullet casings on the deck. "Pick up that brass, Corporal."

"Aye aye sir," Franz replied. *I probably need to shoot this man before we leave the ship. What kind of excuse can I come up with? Do I just cripple him or do the Marines a favor by putting him out of his misery?* The daydream made him feel better. He wanted to write about the incident to Leslie but was afraid someone else might read the letter. If the Lieutenant got killed in battle, the navy would think he had done it. *Better just write about the river trip and the gunboat.*

The Lieutenant called Franz over. "Corporal, have the men start doing some drills and some PT. These men won't act and fight like marines if we don't train them as marines. You're too easy on these men. I want them to be afraid of us more that the enemy. You and your men are wearing marine utility T-shirts. I want them in uniform at all time, including you. You and everyone else are to wear your utility shirts. If we want these men to be marines, they need to look like marines."

"Aye aye sir, I'll take care of that right now." Franz saluted and went to gather the men. *Some of these men have already been in fighting in Nicaragua and here in China. They're very good marines. Any one of them could take on five of that asshole Lieutenant anytime. Having the men do calisthenics in utilities isn't smart. It must be ninety out today. I'll have to watch the men. One of them might kill the Lieutenant before he wises up or before I kill him.*

"All right, jumping jacks," shouted Franz. He counted cadence for the men. "One, two, three, four, five—"

On six, the Captain came out. "At ease, men."

The men stopped. The Captain addressed Franz. "Corporal, it's too hot to exercise out here in utilities. Wait until the sun goes down or have the men strip to their skivvies."

"Which do you want me to do, sir?"

The Lieutenant ran up to Franz without having seen the Captain. "Corporal, what the hell do you think you're doing? Did you quit following my orders again? I'll have you put in irons!" He started drawing his sidearm.

The Captain grabbed the Lieutenant by the shoulder. The Lieutenant whirled around and saw the Captain and the chief glaring at him. "I'm just trying to train these men, sir. They seem to be very lazy and not too much into how we in the military want them to act. This Corporal isn't much of a leader if you ask me, sir. I think he's a jeep."

"Come with me, Lieutenant. We need to talk. Corporal, have your men take off their utility shirts and relax," the Captain said. "Lieutenant, did you look at the personnel files of these men before you got onto my boat?

"No sir. But I know what a marine is supposed to look like and be. My father was the set manager for some Hollywood military films. We always had retired officers as advisers for the movies. A lot of them became family friends. So I know what I'm talking about when I see the enlisted men, sir. We're officers. The enlisted men work for us. They have to obey us. I have a college degree. These enlisted men are deadbeats and dropouts. They need someone to crack the whip on them. I'm not going to let a bunch of low-class enlisted men hurt my marine career."

"Lieutenant, I know more about your men than you do and they're not even mine. I checked on all of them because I always check on the people I have on my boat. Your Corporal is some kind of European aristocrat. He had to leave Europe for dueling. He's killed ten men with his knife since he's been here in China. He's what a marine is supposed to be. Some of his men fought in Nicaragua, and they've all been in combat here in China. These are very well trained and deadly men, Lieutenant. I can't tell you what to do, but you might want to take it easy on your men, and leave my men alone, especially the chief."

"I didn't know any of that sir," replied the Lieutenant.

"You should have, Lieutenant. Next time you get assigned some men, find out who they are. Maybe they'll help you survive if and when we go to war with Japan."

"That's what I'm waiting for, sir, the war. We're going to go through the Japanese like shit through a goose."

"What makes you think that, Lieutenant?"

"Sir, we had plenty of yardmen who were Japanese, and we hired some to be in our movies. I know them. They're small people with bad eyesight. They're lazy and don't take directions very well."

"Lieutenant, the Japanese have over two million men in uniform, five hundred thousand right here in China," the Captain said. "They're pushing the Chinese out of their own country even though the Chinese are armed and backed by the Russians and Americans. The Japanese have also pushed the Brits out of northern China. They're well trained and armed, and they have the will to fight for their emperor. Did you know they have a larger navy in the Pacific than we do? There are only about five hundred marines in China and only fifty-two thousand in the entire military. We do not want the Japanese to go to war with us. We want to stay neutral. Learn from your men, Lieutenant. They know a lot more about this than most of us."

"Aye aye sir," responded the Lieutenant. He was seething with anger at having been told to learn from men well beneath him. He wanted the war to start. He wanted to show the men, the Captain, and the rest of the marines he could lead them to victory. He daydreamed about the medals he would win and the praise of the American people he would get. His dad would make his next war movie about him, the hero marine. He would show them if only the war would start.

The ship docked in Nanping. The Captain ordered the Lieutenant to unload his men and gear. The gunboat would be there for just an hour. He was returning with passengers. "I'll come back for you when you radio me. Give me a day to get here," the Captain said.

"You're not going to wait here?" asked the Lieutenant.

"No, Lieutenant. It's too dangerous to just sit at this dock. You could be gone a week or longer. This boat could make three trips in that time. Our job is to rescue these people. I can't do that waiting on you."

The Lieutenant and his men watched the gunboat leave. "The navy needs to put me in charge of this operation instead of that Captain," the Lieutenant said. "I think he's a coward. While we do the fighting, he's going downstream. All right, Corporal, get the men moving. Let's get off the docks."

"Aye aye sir," Franz said.

He and his men looked around the little town and found four trucks that were out of gas. Their batteries were dead. Franz had his men find other trucks they could cannibalize for batteries, parts, and tires. He wanted to make sure they did not have to abandon a truck before they got back with the civilians they were to rescue.

He had the men fill the trucks with the gas they had brought. They used twelve of the twenty five-gallon cans just to start their trip. Franz realized gas would be a problem before the mission ended. He wanted to make sure they did not waste any fuel on wild goose chases.

The Lieutenant told Franz to take a marine with him in the last truck. The Lieutenant would be in the lead truck with a marine. The other three marines would ride in the two middle trucks with all the gear.

The detail was not very heavily armed. The Lieutenant had a sidearm and a Thompson. Franz had a sidearm and an M-1 Garand. One marine had a Browning automatic rifle, and the other marines had M-1 Garands. Franz made sure each man had three grenades.

The trip across country was not very pleasant. Refugees crowded the roads. Many stalled vehicles and dead livestock blocked the roads. Franz did not see any Japanese soldiers, but he saw many Nationalist and Communist soldiers, both sides heavily armed but not wanting to fight each other. They were going to save their fight for the Japanese if they ran into each other.

The dog rode in the last truck with Franz. It seemed he was going to sleep the entire trip. Franz had to call him a couple of times to make sure he was alive.

The Lieutenant had the convoy pull off the road at an abandoned church and school for the night. Franz had some men prepare chow and others guard the area. He let the dog explore. He figured that if there was any trouble at night, the dog would find it.

The next morning, the Lieutenant decided to have the trucks repacked. He divided all the supplies between the first three trucks. He wanted the radio and the radioman in the back of his truck. He had decided that if they were attacked, the enemy would take out the last truck first, so that truck would not carry any supplies, just the Corporal and the driver. The Lieutenant wanted the radioman to ride on top of the lead truck so he could see farther down the road.

They ate cheese, bread, cake, and water and hit the road. They pulled up to the walled estate where they were to meet their passengers at around noon. Franz sent two marines to scout around, low and quiet. "Take the dog," he told them.

The Lieutenant knocked on the wooden door of the walled estate. The door opened. An American stepped out holding a bible. "Welcome, brother. Are you here to rescue us in the name of God?"

They made plans to leave at dawn the following morning. The Lieutenant went in to help the civilians prepare to leave. Franz and the other marines prepared and ate dinner outside. They slept in the trucks.

The missionaries came out of the house with the Lieutenant and said a prayer to bless their trip. The Lieutenant told the marines to help the people with their cargo and possessions. Franz started loading the trucks. Franz opened one of the boxes he was loading and found it full of red and greed jade statues. He found gold plates, bars, and statues in another. He found pearls and pearl jewelry. It looked to him as if these holy Joes had looted the country. Franz went to the Lieutenant. "Sir, we're getting ready to haul contraband in military vehicles. I think that's illegal."

"Corporal, you're forbidden to look in those crates. They are the religious possessions of the Southern Assembly Church in Alabama and Mississippi. Our job is to get these people safely to an American port. Do I make myself clear, marine?"

"Aye aye sir." Franz saluted and walked away. *I wonder if the Marines would get suspicious if I shot this asshole's kneecap off. I don't think they'll believe me if it happens again. I don't want to think about it. If I do, I'll do it again. He's not caused any real trouble yet. He's just an ass. I need to think about Suzie or read my book on English to German and German to English.*

The road east was crowded. It was as hard going with the traffic as it was going against it. As on the way there, stalled vehicles and dead livestock littered the road. The refugees, who had nothing, were still humiliated by being stripped naked by bandits or Chinese soldiers as they lay dying on the side of the road. The saddest part was that the poor, scared refugees were headed the wrong direction, to the coast, the same place the Japanese were headed. They needed to head west, to the mountains and great plains of China. The Japanese did not have enough men and resources to go that far inland.

The Lieutenant led the convoy off the road to a high, flat area for the noon meal. The missionaries had packed food, so the marines had to fix only their own meals of fruit, bread, cheese, and water. The missionaries had to pray before anyone could eat. Three men gave the noon prayer. That took about twenty minutes.

Thirty-three people were in the missionary party; seventeen were between ages five and eighteen, six of this group were girls between fifteen and eighteen. Seven adult men, nine adult women. The marines were talking and joking with the teenage girls. They reminded Franz of his nieces and nephews in high school, kids talking to kids, no harm being done.

The Lieutenant called Franz over. "Corporal, get your men away from those girls."

"Yes sir. What do you want them to do, sir?"

"I don't want them to do anything. I just want them to stay away from those girls. They're enlisted men, the bottom of the barrel. These girls are from good, Christian-educated stock. Their families deserve better than low-class enlisted men. Do I make myself clear, Corporal?"

"Aye aye sir." Franz saluted and walked away. *Sir, I may not get a chance to shoot you. One or all of the men may do it before I get a chance to.* "Come on, Hopeless. Let's walk the perimeter and see if we're safe."

The convoy was back on the road for an hour and had gone about five miles when the Lieutenant called a halt. A Japanese roadblock was just ahead. The Lieutenant walked back to the last truck and told Franz, "We're going to crash through that roadblock. Be ready."

"Sir, we can't do that. We won't stand a chance."

"Stand a chance? Corporal you're negative and your thoughts are negative. With people like you, I can't win this war."

"Sir, we're not at war with the Japanese or anyone. Sir, we can't crash through that roadblock because they're using a tank to block the road, and it looks like they have a couple dozen well-armed men. They're looking for something or someone. Deserters. Maybe conscripts."

"If you're too scared to fight, Corporal, what is it you want to do?" asked the Lieutenant, loud enough for the civilians with them to hear.

"Sir, I think we should see what they want. They can see us right now. If they were going to jump us, they would have already done it, sir." *Unless they're being led by a dumbass like you.*

"All right, Corporal. Let's get them started toward the roadblock. And remember, you're responsible for any problems. If there's any trouble up there, I'll bust you back to Private. Do I make myself clear, Corporal?"

"Aye aye sir." Franz saluted.

"Corporal, you ride on the running board of my truck until we get though."

"Aye aye sir."

The Japanese stopped the truck. They looked at the marines and the civilians in each truck and waved them through. Franz jumped off the running board and waited until the last truck came up. He climbed into his regular seat.

The rest of the trip was long but uneventful. The convoy got to the dock by seventeen hundred hours. The Lieutenant used the radio to call the boat. The boat was only an hour away, but the Captain told the Lieutenant that they would stay in the middle of the river until morning, that it would be too late to load up and pull out in the dark. They would be sitting ducks for any of the enemy or warlords. The morning would be safer; they could keep the river pirates away from the ship then. "We'll see you in the morning."

This upset the Lieutenant, who stomped around talking about how much of a coward the boat Captain was. He wasn't afraid. He would fight even if he lost all his men and this scaredy-cat naval Captain.

CHAPTER 15

Officer Candidate School

"**M**att, come into my office," called Captain Barious.

"Aye aye sir."

The Captain told Franz to follow him to the Colonel's office because the Colonel wanted to speak to him.

"Aye aye sir," responded Franz.

"Come in, gentleman," said the Colonel when Captain Barious knocked. "Have a seat, men. This is off the record, just us friends having a talk. You guys want a scotch?"

Franz said no. The gunboat Captain, who was on the couch, lifted his glass to Franz and nodded. Franz wondered what was going on.

The Colonel said, "Men, Lieutenant Wiggins has turned the Captain here in for cowardice, and Matt, he's turned you in for failure to follow orders and insubordination. Tell me your stories and how the Lieutenant decided you two should be put out of 'his' military."

The Captain told the story as he knew it. Franz agreed with it. Franz told his story, and the Captain agreed with the part he had been privileged to.

"Thank you, gentleman. Let's meet tonight at the officers' club. I'll buy you men steaks. I think they're serving horse tonight. I'll tell you how all this is going to come out. Matt, Captain Barious needs to see you after this meeting."

"Aye aye sir."

The Captain sat and told Franz to sit. "Matt, the Marine Corps will increase its manpower. It's getting ready to move all the marines out of

China. We need smart and battle-tested officers to help lead and train the new men. Matt, the Colonel wants you to reenlist and go to Officer candidate school in Quantico, Virginia. The Colonel can do this with the stroke of a pen. He just got word that Congress has approved his promotion to General, and he wants you and me on his staff. And yes, I get a gold leaf too. Matt, all you have to do is say yes."

Franz was speechless for a bit. "Sir, do you think I deserve to be an Officer? Sir, am I qualified?"

"Matt, you're the best marine I've ever seen. The Colonel and I trust you with our lives. More than that, we trust you with our Marine Corps."

Franz jumped to attention and saluted. "Yes sir."

That night, Franz wrote to Leslie, Suzie, and Petey Amundus about his good luck. He took Hopeless to Captain Barious and asked him if he would take of the dog until he got back. He flew out of China on a navy PBY bound for the San Diego Naval Air Station. As soon as he signed into San Diego, jotted down the number on a pay phone, and wired it to Otto. The next day, Otto called.

"Hello, my brother! Man, it's good to hear from you. Where are you? You safe?"

"Yes, big brother, I'm safe. I'm passing through San Diego. Otto, I'm on my way to Quantico, Virginia, for the Officer candidate school. I've reenlisted. I'm doing only six weeks of the twelve-week course since I'm already a marine. I'll be in Quantico in six days. Will you have Suzie call me tomorrow same number, same time?"

"Will do, brother."

Suzie called the next day from a pay phone outside the West Asheville Police Department. They spent the first ten minutes saying their I love yous and I've missed yous. Franz asked Suzie, "Will you marry me?"

She screamed. "Yes yes yes!"

"Okay then, this is the plan. I'll turn all this over to Brigitta. She'll keep in touch with you. I love you."

When Otto called later, Franz told him of the good news and gave Otto his idea about the wedding. He asked if Brigitta would arrange the wedding.

"Yes, little brother. Even if we didn't ask her, she'd take over anyway."

"If she does it, it'll be done perfect. Otto, will you tell Daddy for me?"

"Yes, brother, I will."

Franz prepared for Quantico. He got new tailored uniforms. Though he was close to forty, he was in far better shape than the men right out of college.

Most of his classmates were very much like Lieutenant Wiggins—spoiled rich kids who looked down on enlisted men. Franz knew that most of these men would wise up soon enough but that there would be some like the Lieutenant who would just not learn.

Two other men in his class had started out as enlisted men. Both were good marines. The three of them palled around together. They had come to Quantico as brand-new second lieutenants. Instead of taking a week at the firing range, they passed as expert in a couple of hours. Their uniform and marching skills took one hour instead of two weeks.

One week before graduation, Franz started making plans. He was not sure where he would be assigned, but he knew it would be in China with the General and with now Major Barious. But then, the candidates were told that the Marines had been ordered out of China, that the officers who thought they were going to China would be reassigned. Of the eight hundred marines who were then in China, only a hundred and fifty would remain to help close down the American mission there. Franz wondered if Lieutenant Wiggins was coming out of China or staying; he had been reassigned to the Shanghai Fourth Marines when Franz was promoted and sent to Quantico.

Graduation was set for December 4. The marines were in their dress blues on the parade ground. High-ranking officers and dignitaries were on the viewing stand; the graduates' families were lined up on each side of the stand. On the parade field was a marine band, an honor guard, and two hundred marines. The graduates marched to the middle of the field and came to parade rest. Officers and dignitaries gave speeches about honor, marine history, duty, loyalty and being forever faithful.

Otto, Brigitta, Suzie, Daddy Rabbit, and Mattie were applauding and crying and laughing at the same time. Franz marched across the parade field to his family, and they hugged and kissed. The family loaded into the train station bus Otto was using and went to the rail station. Brigitta had arranged for two cabooses for them to travel from Asheville to Quantico. She, Ruth, and Laura Ann had decorated one caboose for the wedding and all the trimmings, including food and a wedding cake.

Otto had arranged for a block of ice to be at the station when they arrived. Daddy Rabbit chipped it up to ice down a case of champagne. Brigitta arranged to have a judge come to the caboose to perform the wedding, which was beautiful and came off without a hitch. Brigitta had done a great job just as everyone knew she would. Otto pulled out a guitar and sang some love songs in high German for the couple. They had great food and a good time.

After the ceremony, Franz told them of his transformation into a marine and how he had gotten to where he was. He told them of his plans to open a restaurant in Hawaii and live near Leslie and his wife as soon as Leslie got her out of China.

Brigitta had gotten Otto and herself the only room left in town because of the graduation. She had fixed the other caboose up as a honeymoon suite. Daddy Rabbit and his lady friend would have to stay in the wedding caboose.

On Friday morning, the cabooses were hooked up to the train, and the wedding party headed for Asheville. Suzie Davis, at that point Mrs. Summers, would stay with Franz at the hotel until Monday and take a train to Asheville. Franz would then stay on the train and eventually end up in San Diego.

Franz and Suzie loved walking around Quantico, visiting the shops and eating at all the little tea and sandwich shops as a married couple. They did not have to hide from anyone. On Sunday morning, Suzie had the pleasure of taking off Franz's second Lieutenant bars and putting on his new first Lieutenant bars.

It was winter and so cold that Suzie would fog up the window in their room with her breath and draw a heart and "I love you" on it. They had their first snowball fight and lay in the snow to make snow angels. Suzie would burst into tears of happiness, and Franz would get misty eyed himself. The had a late brunch and planned to ice skate, something neither had done before. As they got to their hotel, everybody was standing around the radio. Franz asked the bell Captain, "What's up?"

"The Japanese just bombed Pearl Harbor."

Franz said to Suzie, "I don't know what today will bring, but we better be prepared for anything. Let's eat and get packed."

"Why did the Japanese do this?" she asked.

"I'm not sure. It's like the two biggest bullies finally are getting into it."

"Will we win?"

"Sure. It'll be harder and take longer than most people think, but we'll win."

Franz called the camp to see what he was supposed to do. The duty Officer told him to follow his orders and report like normal except sooner than later. Franz told him he would be on the train for the West Coast at oh eight hundreds hours in the morning.

"Good luck, Lieutenant."

Franz and Suzie ate and packed for their first trip as a married couple. That night, they made love with the thought it would be a very long time before they saw each other again if ever. They each had pictures made of each other and together.

The train was full of military men and their families heading south and to the West Coast. Suzie and Franz sat in silence for a while and then began talking softly to each other. Suzie kept hoping the trip would last forever. They hugged and held each other like high school sweethearts. The closer to Asheville they got, the more melancholy Suzie became. She would miss her husband. She was afraid he was going into the fighting.

CHAPTER 16

Parris Island

The train pulled into Asheville. Otto came onboard looking for Franz and Suzie. That surprised Franz.

Otto announced, "I have a wire for Lieutenant Matt Summers" while looking right at Franz.

Franz held up his hand. "Here, sir."

Franz read it. He said to Otto, "Sir, I need to get off this train and catch one to Beaufort, South Carolina. I've been reassigned to the marine training depot at Parris Island."

Suzie asked, "What will you do there?"

"Parris Island Training Depot is the marine basic training facility for the East Coast. I imagine I'll have something to do with training new recruits."

"For how long?"

"Don't know. Maybe until the end of the war. With the Marines, you just can't ever tell."

"Do you think I could move there with you?" said Suzie excitedly.

"Honey, I don't know and will probably not know for a while. Stay here. I'll keep you posted. If I'm going to be assigned to Parris Island for a while, I'll find us a place to live and send for you."

Suzie grabbed Franz's hand. "Let's hope so. If we get to live there, we could start a family."

Otto laughed. "First, let's get off the train, and then we'll figure out how to get you to Beaufort. Do you want to take my car?"

"No, brother, I'll get a car when I get to Parris Island. Marines and navy men are always selling their cars when they ship out. I'll pick up one of those. Find me a train going south. I probably don't need to push my luck here in Asheville. Someone might recognize me."

"Let me get to the dispatcher's office and see what trains are here and where they're going," Otto said. "You two kids just stay in my office until I come back."

Suzie and Franz held hands and kissed for a while. Franz asked, "Suzie, did you tell your mother and father you were marring me?"

"No."

"Why not?"

"I didn't know how to tell them. I couldn't figure out how to work your name into it without scaring them. And I feel it's nobody's business but ours. You're not disappointed in me, are you?"

"Hell no." Franz kissed her. "I haven't figured out how to tell them myself. Dave's a friend of mine, and I don't know how to tell him either. I agree with you. For right now, it's nobody's business but ours. We'll figure out how and when to tell them in the future."

Otto came in. "Let's go, big boy. A train is coming in from Tennessee right now with marine recruits. It'll be picking up recruits in Greenville, Newberry, Lexington, Columbia, and Orangeburg all the way to Parris Island."

"I reckon I'll board that train."

"Brother, what is your job in the Marines? What exactly do you do?"

"Frankly, big brother, I don't know. I'm a combat marine. All I know is combat and cooking, and I'm pretty sure they aren't sending me to Parris Island to cook. I'll have to wait until I get there and see."

Franz had to run to catch his train. It was full of young and very eager men. Franz walked in the train car in a class-A uniform with ribbons and campaign pins. He looked sharp. He sat in the club car and ordered a Coke and some peanuts. He made sure to speak with all the officers he saw there.

The ride to Parris Island was slow. The train was crowded. The men sang and played musical instruments. Everybody was upbeat. A few marine officers had also already seen combat and could tell by how Franz talked and carried himself that he had been in combat also.

Franz had to sleep in the club car. After breakfast, he went to the car with showers and toilets. Franz had a long shower, shaved, brushed his teeth, and put on a fresh uniform and shined shoes. He was ready to meet the new day and its adventures.

He noticed that most of these young men had not showered, shaved, or cleaned up; they looked unkempt, sloppy. Franz laughed to himself. *Young men, I'd like to see you after a tough drill Sergeant gets hold of you.*

At the camp, he reported to the duty Officer. He was told to report to the base's Officer quarters and then at thirteen hundred hours to the base Commander's office at the end of the quad.

When Franz went to the base Commander's office to report in, he saw four other young officers with the Commander, Major Barious.

"It's good to see you again, Matt," said the Major as he shook Franz's hand.

"Good to see you, sir," replied Franz.

"Matt, let me introduce you to your fellow officers, Lieutenant David West, Second Lieutenant Al Sheppard, Lieutenant Bob Potts, and you already know Lieutenant M. E. Gray."

"Yes sir," said Franz. He shook their hands and said to Lieutenant Gray, "Good to see you again, Lieutenant."

"Please call me Bob, Matt."

"Gentlemen, let's get started," said the Major. "I know you're wondering why you're here. It's because each of you has a skill we need you to teach to the marines when they go to their advanced training schools. You all have seen some overseas combat. You need to pass your survival skills on to these young boys. Matt, you're going to be the hand-to-hand combat specialist. David, you're the stealth expert. I want these men to learn to be invisible in the field. Al, you're the survival expert. I want these men to know how to eat and what to eat, how to find food and water or how to live without either. M. E., you're the demolitions expert. I want them to be able to blow up whatever they have to. Bob, you're a communications expert. These men need to know how to get and stay in contact with us.

"Gentlemen, the first of the marine recruits will be finished with basic training in a week. That's how long you have to set up your classes.

You have these men for a week for each class. You have to focus your efforts on getting these men ready for battle. They'll be only as good as we train them to be. Any questions?"

Franz and his new colleagues started their advanced combat training classes. They transferred in clerks and office staff. They transferred in some combat-trained sergeants as instructors. Lieutenant Gray told the other lieutenants of how Franz had walked through the roughnecks in Tucson, breaking bones and throwing them around as if they were rag dolls. He told the others about Franz's reputation for hand-to-hand fighting in China and the number of men he had killed. He told them of the missions Franz had been on and how successful they had been. The Lieutenant told the others that if they went into fighting, the best place to be was beside Lieutenant Matt Summers.

The training school was training the recruits in the basic skills of staying alive, but Franz knew this type of school needed to be much longer for these boys, some of them who had been raised in regular, middle-class families. They had been brought up in nice neighborhoods by loving parents. They had to be taught to be hard, to take life without thinking, to give their lives without thinking.

After six weeks of training, Franz rented a small apartment in Beaufort, South Carolina, and Suzie moved down with him. She told her parents she had met a marine from California and was marrying him that week in South Carolina. She said her new name would be Suzie Summers.

Franz and Suzie set up housekeeping. Franz had friends over once a week for some good Swiss or German food. Major Barious and his wife were regulars at the Summerses, and the couples fished together. There was always a bridge game. Franz had never realized he could play cards without gambling and have a good time. Suzie loved to show her husband off at the officers' club dances. Franz danced like a professional, and all the older women wanted to dance with him.

The United States and Great Britain were not faring well in the Pacific. The Japanese were taking island after island without being stopped. The Americans needed a victory for the sake of morale. It had had two victories—the Makin Island raid and the Jimmy Doolittle raid on mainland Japan, neither of which had done any real damage to property or the war machine, but they had given the Americans a morale boost. The Marines were assigned the operations at Guadalcanal, in the Solomon Islands. It controlled a large portion of the Pacific. From the airfields on Guadalcanal, most of the islands in that part of the ocean could be controlled.

Suzie and Franz decided he would stay in the Marines and retire and then open their restaurant in Hawaii. They planned a weekend of fishing and cookouts with other marine and navy families on the barrier islands at Beaufort. Franz was going to make his Beaufort stew—corn on the cob, whole, small red potatoes, Italian link sausages, crab claws, large shrimp, and lots of spices. He and Suzie were going to give it a German name for their restaurant and call it Swiss food.

Thursday morning at oh seven hundred hours was commanders' call. All the officers and the higher-ranking NCOs had to attend. "Gentleman, this is General Marcus Adams. He's going to lead the invasion at Tulagi on the Solomon Islands. He is choosing the bulk of his fighting force from here and from Cherry Point. Each man will receive orders telling him where he will be assigned. The Marines have men from convalescent leave coming in to take your place. Your troop train will leave here Sunday at noon, Monday at noon, and Tuesday at noon. Those men with families here need to make arrangements now. Dismissed."

Franz told Suzie of the news. He called Otto and found out he could ride with Suzie home and meet one of the troop trains in Kansas City. He and Suzie would have to leave Sunday at noon to make his connections. "Suzie you start packing. I have to find the Major to see if he will let me do this."

Franz went to the Major's home and found him talking to his wife. "Sir, may I have a minute of your time?" Franz asked. "Hello, Katherine. It's nice to see you."

"Nice to see you, Matt. How's Suzie?" she asked. "What does she think of these orders?"

"She's not too pleased."

"Matt, let's talk out in the garden," the Major said. "Dear, I'll be in in a few minutes."

Franz and the Major walked to the vegetable garden.

"Major, I need your permission to board our troop train on Monday in Kansas City. My brother Otto can get me on a train that will be in Kansas City the same time as our train. He'll make sure our train does not leave without me. This way, I can ride home with Suzie to her parents' home in Asheville."

"Strange. I always thought she was from California," the Major said. "Matt, I trust you. I know you'll be there. Give my best to Miss Suzie. I'll see you in Missouri."

"Thank you sir." Franz saluted and walked away.

On Friday, Franz and Suzie packed and sold all the household items they weren't taking. They sold their like-new '35 Olds to an older top gunnery Sergeant; it had been a good car for them. That evening, the Major had a cocktail party for his officers and their ladies.

On Saturday, Franz turned in all the base equipment he had been assigned and signed off base. That night, he and Suzie ate and danced at the officers' club and skinny-dipped in the ocean for the last time for a long while.

Sunday morning, Franz ate breakfast with his men who were not going overseas. He made his version of SOS—something or other on a shingle, which was toast—for them with eggs over easy.

Franz and Suzie boarded their train that Sunday evening for Asheville. Suzie wanted a baby; she and Franz did their best in that respect on the train late at night. They could hear the wheels clicking on the rails and the road crossings. They drank champagne and stayed in bed in the sleeper car almost all the way to Asheville.

The train pulled into Asheville early Monday morning. Otto, Brigitta, and Daddy Rabbit greeted them at the station. Daddy Rabbit and Otto unloaded their luggage and belongings. Otto put Franz's military luggage on the train headed to Kansas City. Franz and Suzie had one hour together before his train pulled out.

CHAPTER 17

Guadalcanal

The train to Kansas City was over half filled with military. Most of the men were navy; others were army, and some were marines. Franz wandered around until he came to the club car, which was full of officers. He played bridge with two navy and three army officers all the way to Kansas City. A few of them could have been tournament bridge players; they were smart and could read the other players, Franz found that he had to focus hard to stay even with them. He liked the competition; it made the time go by, and he exercised his brain.

The trip took twenty-four hours. They got to Kansas City early Tuesday morning. The train was headed to San Diego; Franz needed a train to San Francisco. He got off the train and heard the announcement that the train to San Francisco was boarding. He grabbed his luggage and had just boarded it when it pulled out. He had to find his men and his officers. He started in the club car and found the Major and the other officers he was assigned to.

Barious laughed. "I just made some money. Some of these guys didn't think you'd make the connection. Your train was supposed to get here after this train left, but for some reason, our train sat on the tracks for a half hour. Did your brother have anything to do with that?"

Franz laughed. "I really don't know. I do know that all these railroad men stick together and always help each other out, so maybe."

Franz wrote letters to Suzie and Otto. He played cards and napped all the way to San Francisco. The men had one night in San Francisco.

They boarded older passenger ships that were serving as troop ships and headed for Hawaii.

The marines onboard were going to Hawaii and be the second wave of marines to hit the beach at Tulagi on Guadalcanal. As soon as Franz's ship docked in Hawaii, he called Leslie. Leslie picked him up at the marine barracks and took him to Alma and Woodley Patton's home to meet them and enjoy a Hawaiian, home-cooked meal. Franz was delighted to meet the Pattons. They talked about the Marines and about life in Hawaii. Franz told them of his and Suzie's plans to retire out of the Marines and relocate to Hawaii to open a restaurant. Suzie would be the pastry chef and Franz would be the head chef. He told them about the recipes he was working on and how he would substitute local vegetables for traditional Swiss or German vegetables. They all had a great time. Franz was really beginning to understand the closeness of a good family, he felt blessed.

On his last night in Hawaii, Franz cooked for the Pattons, Leslie, and the officers in his company. The Major had eaten Franz's cooking many times. He asked Franz make his favorite, German pork chops and sauerkraut and Swiss potato roesti with leeks. He made pineapple and cherry strudel for dessert. They drank a dark German beer and told funny stories about basic training. The young officers were nervous; they needed to see that their higher-ranking officers were not.

Training was long and hard, but the men took to it. They had been trained to assault a larger force and were ready for that. In two weeks, the marines shipped out again, this time for action. They spent the next week training and staying in shape. They had physicals and classes on Japanese. They had target practice and shooting competitions onboard the ships.

Guadalcanal was a beautiful atoll in the Pacific. The men could see it from many miles out but could not tell it from any other island until they got nearer and saw lots of fighters flying over it. They realized the fighters were engaging in dogfights. They saw artillery shells exploding.

The order came to start loading onto the landing crafts. Each man was to check his weapons and gear. The landing crafts left the troop ships. The water was extremely rough. Maybe the flat-bottomed boats made it seem rough. Franz was halfway back in his landing craft and was feeling seasick.

"Get ready!" came the call.

The men got into charging positions. As soon as the front of the landing craft dropped, the men ran off and spread out.

"Get off the beach!" came the call.

Franz was running and motioning his men to follow him. As soon as he got to the seagrass, he dropped. That was when he realized they were not taking any fire. Their landing had been soft compared to the morning landings he had heard about. He grouped his men and found the Major. The Major told them they were to move inland as far as they could before nightfall.

Franz moved his men into the groves off the beach. He had them dig in and make ready for nightfall. They could hear a lot of gunfire around them, but so far, they were not in any of the conflict.

At oh two hundred hours, the Japanese tried to push the Americans off of the island. The fighting was furious. It was dark, and it was hard to just fire away into the jungle because the Americans were not sure where the Japanese were and where the Americans were.

Franz got his men regrouped and pointed in the right direction. They dug in again and decided to not be overrun. Franz told his men to pick their targets, to make each shot count. Franz had the strangest thought. *I wish the dog were here.* His men put out a steady string of fire and hit about everything they shot at.

The morning broke. The Major came to Franz's position to check everything out. "Lieutenant, you and your men did a great job. Your group seems to have broken the back of their charge. You all rest. We're sure they'll hit us again tonight, only more of them, so be prepared. Any casualties?"

"Yes sir. Four wounded, one pretty bad, sir,"

"You were lucky, Lieutenant. We took a lot of casualties last night," replied the Major. "We're sending in some replacements at noon. Show them what to do and how to do it your way, Matt."

"Yes sir."

Franz sent a couple of men for ammunition and grenades and others for chow for his company. He knew he could have hot food during the day but not at night; no fires. Evening chow would be cold.

As night fell, Franz's men were beginning to take small-arms fire. Later in the evening, the Japanese fired more at the Americans. It began to rain. The men were hungry, wet, and exhausted. By midnight, they were in a downpour eating wet food. But the men relaxed, thinking the weather was as bad for the Japanese as it was for them.

At oh two hundred hours, the Japanese charged. It was so dark that the Americans had trouble seeing the Japanese at any distance. The fighting became hand-to-hand. Many on both sides were killed. Franz was at his best in hand-to-hand combat. He used his skills with a knife and his hawk-billed knife to slit the throats of five Japanese. His men saw most of this and felt safe in his company.

The fighting lasted until about oh five hundred hours. It stopped raining. The Japanese stopped their charge. Franz had lost 40 percent of his men. Half were dead and half were wounded. *I understand why men love war. I love the fighting too. I think I like the killing too much. I just don't like ordering men to die. I trained them the best I could, but I still lost too many good boys. I have to protect them better. I have to get my men the hell out of here.*

The fighting went on for days. For weeks. Franz's company was taking casualties daily, mostly wounded but some dead. The Major had a company Officer meeting to discuss new plans coming in from headquarters. After the meeting was over, when the officers were headed back to their companies, Franz, another Officer and the Major were attacked by the Japanese, who were looking for officers to capture to get information.

The Japanese were lucky. They had captured a Major and two lieutenants. The Japanese made their captives drop their weapons and weapon belts. They tied the Major's hands behind his back and tried tying the Lieutenant's hands. Franz pulled out a knife with his left and. He fumbled it. He cursed. One Japanese soldier grinned and bent to pick it up. Franz cut his throat with his hawk-billed knife, spun, got another soldier by the hair, and cut his throat. Franz grabbed the man's rifle and killed Japanese number three. He stuck number four with his own bayonet.

Franz untied his Major and the other Officer. They collected their weapons and headed to their companies.

On the way back, the Lieutenant said to the Major, "Did you see that? He killed those men before they knew they were dead. Did you see how fast he was, sir?"

"Yes. That's why he's with us. He's the best marine on this damn island."

That afternoon, the Major put Franz in for the marine Silver Star.

Franz briefed his men on the job for the night. He had been informed that the Marines thought the Japanese would try another Major offense that night. The men needed to be awake and on guard during what would be a very long night. The Japanese could not give up Guadalcanal to the Americans. 'Canal was too close to all the shipping lanes and Japan itself. The Americans could launch all their bombing raids from 'Canal and cripple the Japanese throughout the Pacific.

Franz made sure his men slept in shifts and had some hot chow before the fighting was to begin. He made sure his men had plenty of ammunition and water. They could hear fighting all around them. It was coming closer. He told his aide to fire some flares, which lit up the dark sky. They saw hundreds of Japanese advancing on their position. He dropped to his knee and ordered his men to fire. He had to stop the advance. His men fought valiantly. They held off three charges. The marines were outnumbered but not outfought.

When the fighting ended, the sun was rising. Franz saw hundreds of Japanese and American dead. The medics were trying to help the wounded. The marines looked completely worn out. Franz saw the Major walking toward him about a hundred yards out. Franz had a .45 automatic in one hand and his hawk-billed knife in the other. He was covered in blood, ash, dirt, sweat. But his men had done well. He raised his hand to the Major the same time a Japanese mortar round exploded behind him.

CHAPTER 18

Wounded but Alive

Franz woke up in a hospital ship in the China Sea. It took him a few minutes to figure out where he was. He felt himself and found he was missing no body parts. The last thing he remembered was waving to the Major at the conclusion of the Japanese attack.

A corpsman told him he had been wounded and had been in a coma for a couple of days, three to be exact. He said that Franz would be okay, that he had a couple of new holes in him but nothing to make him look bad. The corpsman told Franz that the marines had won the battle and everything was quiet on the Canal at the time.

Franz asked where he was headed. The corpsman told him he was a few days from Pearl Harbor.

Franz went back to sleep.

He spent the next week sailing to Pearl Harbor. He was taken to the naval hospital. He had a nurse call Leslie and tell him where he was. Leslie and the Pattons came to see him. Leslie wired his dad about him. Franz wrote to Suzie, Daddy Rabbit, and Otto to let them know he was all right and would be in the hospital for only a short time more. He could not come home but would be conversing with Leslie.

Seven days later, Franz was signed out of the hospital. He had been promoted to the rank of Captain effective two days earlier. Leslie and the Pattons came to take him home. They shook his hand and saluted.

As soon as he left the hospital and was walking to their car, the shore patrol came up and announced he was under arrest. They cuffed him. The Pattons laughed, thinking it was a joke being played by Leslie. But when they saw Franz's face, they knew something was wrong.

"I'll go with you," Leslie said. "Alma, Woodley, I'll call you later." He climbed into the front of the truck with a guard.

When they got to the stockade, the provost marshal said, "Sorry, Captain. We were ordered to put you in the brig. I just heard about your being awarded the Silver Star and getting your bars. I'm not sure why you're here. I looked up your record. You're an excellent marine."

"Thank you, Commander. I won't be any trouble. May I talk to my nephew here for a bit?"

"Sure, Chief. Let me know when you're ready to leave."

"Leslie, wire your dad. Tell him what's happened. Tell him that I need to figure this out and will let him know what I need. Please have him tell Suzie and Daddy Rabbit. They don't need to do anything until I let them know what I need. You do know what this is about, don't you, Leslie? Or at least what you think it's about?"

"I think so, Franz. Something that happened about four years ago when you left Asheville."

"I think so," said Franz. "Damn. It took four years to catch me. I wonder why now."

THE END OF BOOK TWO.
LOOK FOR BOOK THREE SOON.

Fictional Characters in This Novel

Herbert Charles: patriarch of the Charles family; born in Switzerland, 1875; brought his family to America, 1906
Stella Carter: married Herbert Charles, 1910
Otto Charles: Herbert's oldest son, 1896
John Charles: secondborn son of Herbert, 1899
Etta Charles: only daughter of Herbert, 1901
Franz Charles: youngest son of Herbert, 1904
Brigitta Miesenhamer: married Otto Charles, 1916
Leslie Charles: first son of Otto, 1920
Albert Charles: second son of Otto, 1924
John Henry Charles: third son of Otto, 1926
Frank Charles: fourth son of Otto, 1927
Ava Charles: first daughter of Otto, 1929
Sonja Charles: second daughter of Otto, 1930
Herbert Charles: youngest son of Otto, 1932

Colonel Marcus Adams: Colonel of the marines in China
Petus "Petey" Amundus: second Lieutenant in China
Colonel Amundus: father of Lieutenant Amundus
Captain Barious: marine Captain for whom Franz is aide
*Steve Bellich: draftsman
Buddy Bryant: gambler friend of Franz
Ray Davis: Suzie Davis's husband
Suzie Davis: Franz's woman friend

*Aubrey Giezentanner: college girlfriend of Albert

Charles M. E. Gray: marine second Lieutenant

Mr. and Mrs. Hamilton: minister and wife in Johnson City

*Hojoh: rickshaw driver in China

Bob Jolly: marine Lieutenant

Don Jones: Asheville chief of police

*Lechou: Chinese girl

*Lieutenant JG MacConnel: XO of USS *Guam*

Alice Mauney: PhD student at LSU

*Martin McCracken: JAG Officer

Dave Morris: Suzie Davis's brother, friend of Franz

*Mr. Noble: teacher at Lee Edwards High School

Daddy Rabbit (Isaiah Green): best friend of Franz, patriarch of the Green family, bar and gambling club owner

Mattie Blue: daughter of the bartender at Daddy Rabbit's club, the go-between for Suzie and Franz

Ruth: colored maid and cook for the Charles family

Laura Ann: Ruth's sister and laundry maid for Brigitta Charles

Mrs. Bagwell: boarder of Charles family and elderly schoolteacher

*Mr. Carter: boarder and druggist

*Mrs. Carter: boarder and wife of Mr. Carter; nurse at Anderson Hospital

*George Coppersmith: navy teletype operator

*Charles David: navy welder

John Greene: colored French chef at La Parisienne Restaurant

Maude Kennedy: woman from Great Lakes

Joe McGhee: chief petty Officer, welder, Leslie's best friend in China

*J. D. Moore: navy Lieutenant junior grade

Mr. O'Kelly: butcher at Mrs. Johnson's store

Katie Scrounce: teacher and lady friend of Leslie

Mrs. Scrounce: Katie's mother, a teacher

*Billy Smith: petty Officer third class welder who talked Leslie into joining the navy

*Alex Taft: federal marshal

*Emery Tanner: Captain, USS *Guam*
*Joseph Weeks: navy Captain
William Wiggins: marine Lieutenant
*Gay Woody: navy fireman

Printed in the United States
By Bookmasters